EARTH
WAS
FRAFFIN'S WORLD

Fraffin's sensory movies had provided the Chem surcease from eternal boredom, and so his storyship empire
was soon infamous in the Chem universe. But now Kelexel
had come to Fraffin's world to destroy it.

Somehow, in some way that great entrepreneur-cum-
movie producer was disobeying the laws of the Primacy—
and Kelexel's job was to find out how.

Was the storyship king selling his creatures for pets?
Were his people openly fraternizing with the planet-bound
Earthlings? Or was secret knowledge being passed to
those mere mortals? Kelexel was sure the crime was one of
these ... the signs of secrecy were everywhere.

But Fraffin's movies were getting better and better—
and what Kelexel didn't know was that soon he himself
would have a starring role in one of the master's finest and
most dangerous premeditated dramas of love ... and
death!

Publisher's Note: This novel was originally published in 1968.
In the intervening years the author has found portions of
the novel which he believed could be improved; and so, he
has rewritten these sections for this edition.

Also by Frank Herbert:

DUNE

DUNE MESSIAH

CHILDREN OF DUNE

EYES OF HEISENBERG

THE GOD MAKERS

GREEN BRAIN

HELLSTROM'S HIVE

SANTAROGA BARRIER

SOUL CATCHER

*THRESHOLD: The Blue Angels Experience

*UNDER PRESSURE

WHIPPING STAR

*Published by Ballantine Books

THE
HEAVEN
MAKERS

Frank Herbert

A Del Rey Book

BALLANTINE BOOKS • NEW YORK

A Del Rey Book
Published by Ballantine Books

Copyright © 1968, 1977 by Frank Herbert

All rights reserved. Published in the United States by Ballantine Books, a division of Random House, Inc., New York, and simultaneously in Canada by Ballantine Books of Canada, Ltd., Toronto, Canada.

A somewhat different version of this novel was serialized in the April and June 1967 issues of *Amazing Stories,* copyright © 1967 by Ultimate Publishing Co.

ISBN 0-345-30290-7

Manufactured in the United States of America

First Ballantine Books Edition: March 1977
Third Printing: April 1982

Cover art by Darrell K. Sweet

"Every man is as Heaven made him, and sometimes a great deal worse."

—Miguel de Cervantes

1

FULL OF FOREBODINGS AND THE GREATEST TENSIONS
that an adult Chem had ever experienced, Kelexel the
Investigator came down into the storyship where it hid
beneath the ocean. He pressed his slender craft
through the barrier that stood like lines of insect legs in
the green murk and debarked on the long gray landing
platform.

All around him flickering yellow discs and globes of
working craft arrived and departed. It was early daylight topside and from this ship Fraffin the Director
was composing a story.

To be here, Kelexel thought. *Actually to be on
Fraffin's world.*

He felt that he knew this world intimately—all those
hours before the pantovive watching Fraffin's stories
about the place unroll before his eyes. Background
study for the investigation it'd been called. But what
Chem wouldn't have traded places with him then—
gladly?

To be on Fraffin's world!

That morning topside—he had seen such mornings
many times, caught by Fraffin's shooting crews: the
torn sky, cloud-pillars of gilded cushions. And the
creatures! He could almost hear a priestmother mur-
muring, her voice firmly hesitant before a Chem posing
as a god. Ah, such buttersoft women they were, gener-
ous with their barbed kisses.

But those times were gone—except for Fraffin's
reels. The creatures of this world had been herded into
new avenues of excitement.

In the pangs of remembering Fraffin's stories, Kelexel
recognized his own ambivalence.

I must not weaken, he thought.

There was an element of grandiose posturing in the thought (hand on breast) and Kelexel permitted an inward chuckle at himself. Fraffin had done that for him. Fraffin had taught many a Chem a great deal about himself.

In spite of the confusion on the landing platform, the Dispatcher noted Kelexel almost immediately and sent a hovering robot questioner before whose single eye Kelexel bowed and said: "I am a visitor, Kelexel by name."

He did not have to say he was a rich visitor. His craft and his clothing said that for him. The clothing was the quiet forest green of neversoil and cut for comfort: leotards, a simple tunic and an all-purpose cape. It gave his squat, bow-legged form a look of rich dignity, setting off the silvery Chem-of-Chem skin, forcing attention onto the big face with its rock like angles and planes, the sunken and penetrating brown eyes.

The craft which he left in a rest slot beneath the traffic lanes for the working crews was a needleship which could stitch its way across any void in the Chem universe. Only the wealthiest entrepreneurs and Servants of the Primacy owned such ships. Even Fraffin didn't possess one, preferring (so it was said) to plow his wealth back into the world which had brought him such fame.

Kelexel, a visitor—he felt confidence in the cover. The Bureau of Criminal Repression had prepared his role and trappings with care.

"Welcome, visitor Kelexel," the Dispatcher said, his voice amplified through the robot to override the storyship activity. "Take the flex ramp on your left. Please register with our Greeter at the head of the ramp. May your stay with us relieve boredom."

"My gratitude," Kelexel said.

Ritual, everything was ritual, he thought. *Even here.*

He fitted his bowed legs to the riding clamps. The ramp whisked him across the platform, up through a red hatch, along a blue passageway to a glistening ebony orifice. The orifice expanded to reveal a small room and the Greeter's flashing lights, couch and dangling connections.

Kelexel eyed the robo-couplings, knowing they must be linked to the storyship's Central Directory. Here was the true moment of test for his cover, the heart of Ship Security.

The tensions boiling in him filled Kelexel with sudden wonder. He felt no fear for his person; under his skin—part of his skin—lay the web armor which immunized all Chem from violence. It was improbable that they could harm him. Something approaching the entire Chem civilization was required to harm an individual. Such decisions came rarely and then only because of a clear and positive threat to all Chem.

But four previous investigators had come here and returned to report "no crime" when all surface evidence pointed to something profoundly wrong in Fraffin's private empire. Most disquieting was the fact that all four had left the Service to start their own storyships out on the rims.

Kelexel held this knowledge to him now, secure in the Chem *oneness*, the shared unity that Tiggywaugh's web gave each Chem with his immortality.

I'm ready for you, Greeter, he thought.

He already knew the Primacy's suspicions must be correct. Senses trained to respond to the slightest betrayal recorded more than enough here to bring him to full alert. Signs of decadence he'd expected. Storyships were outposts and outposts tended that way. But there was a surfeit of other symptoms. Certain of the crew moved with that air of knowledgeable superiority which flashed like a warning light to the police eye. There was a casual richness of garb on even the lowliest menials. There was a furtive something here which oozed from the oneness of the web.

He'd seen inside several of the working craft, noted the silver sheen on handles of concealment controls. The creatures of this world had long since passed the stage where Chem could legally reveal themselves on the surface. It was one thing to nudge and herd and manipulate intelligent creatures for the sake of entertainment—"to relieve boredom"—quite another thing to sow the seeds of an awareness that could explode *against* the Chem.

No matter Fraffin's fame and stature, he'd taken a wrong turning somewhere. That was obvious. The stupidity of such an action put a sour taste in Kelexel's mouth. No criminal could escape the Primacy's endless searching—not forever.

Still, this was Fraffin's storyship—Fraffin who had given the Chem surcease from immortal boredom, given them a world of profound fascination in story after story.

He felt those stories in his memory now, sensed the ringing of old bells, their sound falling, lingering, falling—the parapets of awareness roaring there to willy-nilly purpose. Ahhh, how Fraffin's creatures caught the mind! It was in part their similarity to the Chem, Kelexel felt. They made one disregard their gigantism. They forced one to identify with their dreams and emotions.

Remembering, remembering, Kelexel heard the music of bowstrings, warcries and whimpers, kite-shadowed silences on bloody fields—all Fraffin's doing. He remembered a fair Gutian female, a slave being marched to Babylon in the time of Cambyses—an Egyptian woman taken with her child.

The spoil of the bow, Kelexel thought, recalling the sweep of that one story. One lost female, yet how she lingered in his memory. She had been sacrificed before Nin-Girsu who blessed commerce and litigation and was in reality the voice of a Chem Manipulator in Fraffin's pay.

But here were names and creatures and events the Chem would never have known were it not for Fraffin. This world, Fraffin's storyship empire, had become a byword in the Chem universe. It would not be easy (nor popular) to topple such a one, but Kelexel could see that it must be done.

I must destroy you, Kelexel thought as he coupled himself to the Greeter. He stared with quiet interest up at the scanners which flowed across him, searching, searching. This was normal and to be expected from Ship Security. To be a Chem immortal was to submit to this as a matter of course. There could be no threat to any Chem except from his fellow Chem united—and the Chem could be united by false ideas as well as true ones. False assumptions, fantastic plots—only the Primacy was supposed proof against such base maneuvers. Fraffin had to satisfy himself that the visitor wasn't a competitor's spy intending secret harm.

How little you know of harm, Kelexel thought as he felt the Greeter probe him. *I need only my senses and my memory to destroy you.*

He wondered then what specific criminal act would trip up Fraffin. Was he breeding some of his creatures for short stature, selling them as pets? Were his people openly fraternizing with their planet-bound giants? Was secret knowledge being fed to the creatures? They did, after all, have crude rockets and satellites. Was theirs an unreported *infectious* intelligence, full of immunes, ready to blast out into the universe and oppose the Chem?

It must be one of these, Kelexel thought. The signs of secrecy were all here on Fraffin's world. There was guilty knowledge in the storyship.

Why would Fraffin do such a stupid thing? Kelexel wondered. *The criminal!*

2

THE GREETER'S REPORT CAME TO FRAFFIN WHERE HE sat at his pantovive editing the latest rushes on his current story.

The war, the war, the lovely little war, he was thinking.

And oh, how Chem audiences loved the effect of flamelighted nights, the naked panting of these creatures in their mortal struggles. One of their leaders reminded him of Cato—the same eternally ancient features, the cynical glaze of inward-drinking eyes. Cato, now . . . there'd been a grand story.

But the pantovive's three-dimensional images faded, the tracing light receded before the priority of a message, and there was Ynvic's face staring at him, her bald head glistening under the lights in her surgery, her heavy brows arched in a quizzical frown.

"A visitor calling himself Kelexel has arrived," she said. (And Fraffin, watching the flash of her teeth, the heavy lips, thought: *She's overdue for rejuvenation*.) "This Kelexel most likely is the Investigator we've been expecting," she added.

Fraffin straightened, uttered a curse that'd been popular on his world in the time of Hasdrubal: "Bal, burn their seed!" Then: "How certain are you?"

"The visitor is a visitor to perfection," Ynvic said. She shrugged. "He is too perfect. Only the Bureau could be that perfect."

Fraffin settled back into his editing chair. She was probably correct. The Investigator's timing was about right. Out in the Chem universe they didn't have this feeling for the nicety of timing. Time ran at such a crazy speed for most Chem. But association with the

6

creatures of this world imparted a pseudosense of time. Yes, it was probably the Investigator.

He looked up and around at his silver-walled salon-office in the heart of the storyship. This long low place crammed with creative machinery and the devices of relaxation usually remained insulated from transient planetary distractions. As a rule, only Ynvic dared disturb him at his work here. She would not do it lightly. Something about this visitor, Kelexel, had alerted her.

Fraffin sighed.

Even through the storyship's sophisticated barriers and the deeps of ocean in which they hid, he often felt that he could sense the passage of the planet's sun and moon and that troubles waited for the worst conjunctions to plague him.

Waiting behind him on his desk was a report from Lutt, his Master-of-Craft, that new three-man shooting crew, youngsters of promise all, had been out on the surface with shields down letting the natives see them, stirring up a storm of local speculation. Teasing the natives was, of course, an ancient diversion with the Chem of this storyship.

But not now.

Why did they choose this partcular moment? he wondered.

"We'll throw this Kelexel a sop," he said. "The shooting crew that was out teasing the natives. Dismissal for all of them and for the dispatcher who allowed them to surface without an old hand as guide."

"They may talk," Ynvic said.

"They don't dare," he said. "Anyway, explain what's happened and send them along with recommendations to one of the new ships. I hate to lose them, but. . . ." He shrugged.

"Is that all you're going to do?" Ynvic asked.

Fraffin passed a hand over his eyes, scratched his left brow. Her meaning was clear, but he hated to abandon the lovely little war. He stared into the glittering shell of the pantovive where his memory still held the lingering images of violence. If he pulled out his Manipulators, the natives likely would settle their differences across a conference table. They had that tendency more and more of late.

Again, he thought of the problems awaiting him at his desk. There was the memo from Albik, the story-chief, the usual complaint: "If you wish me to cover this much story action *simultaneously* then I must have more skimmers and platforms, more shooting crews, more cutting-room operators . . . more . . . more . . . more . . ."

Fraffin longed for the good old days when Birstala had been his storychief. There was a man capable of making his own decisions when the equipment and crews wouldn't stretch. But Birstala had succumbed to the immortal nemesis, boredom. He had his own story-ship now with the seed from this planet and his own world somewhere off beyond the beyond. He had his own problems.

"Maybe you should sell out," Ynvic said.

He glared at her. "That's impossible and you know why!"

"The right buyer. . . ."

"Ynvic!"

She shrugged.

Fraffin pushed himself out of the editing chair, crossed to his desk. Its immersed viewscreen showed the discus galaxies and variable stars of the Chem birthworlds. A touch of the controls and this scene vanished to present a view from space looking down on their private little planet, this blue-green world with its patterns of clouds over seas and continents, the sharp flakes of star cosmos beyond.

His own features lay there suddenly reflected in the desk's polished surface as though swimming out of the planet: the sensual mouth in a straight line, nostrils flared in his narrow hooked nose, dark eyes brooding under overhanging brows, the high forehead with twin coves of silvery Chem flesh in the short black hair.

Ynvic's face came through the Central Directory's message center relays to dance above the desk and stare at him expectantly.

"I've given my opinion," she said.

Fraffin looked up at the Shipsurgeon, a bald, roundfaced Chem of the Ceyatril breed—old, old even by Chem standards—extravagant with age. A thousand stars such as the sun which whirled this planet in its loop of gravity could have been born and died in the life of Shipsurgeon Ynvic. There were rumors she'd been a planet buyer once and even a member of the Larra crew which had probed the other dimensions. She wouldn't say, naturally, but the story persisted.

"I can never sell my world, Ynvic," he said. "You know that."

"A Chem is wise to avoid the word never," she said.

"What do our sources say about this Kelexel?" he asked.

"That he's a rich merchant, recently allowed to breed, favored by the Primacy."

"And you think he's the new snooper."

"I think it."

If Ynvic thinks it, then it's probably true, he thought.

He knew he was stalling, vacillating. He didn't want to drop the lovely little war and gear the ship to meet this new threat.

Perhaps Ynvic's right, he thought. *I've been here too long, eaten too much identification with our poor, ignorant natives.*

Another snooper from the Bureau come to watch us!

And what the man sought could not be hidden long. Ynvic was saying that to him with every word and gesture.

I should abandon this planet, he thought. *How did I absorb so much identification with these gross, stupid savages? We don't even share death in common. They die; we don't.*

I've been one of their gods!

What if this snooper cannot be tempted?

Damn the Bureau!

"He's not going to be an easy one, this Investigator," Ynvic said. "He poses as one of the very rich. If he bids on the ship why not confound them—sell out. What could they do? You could plead ignorance; the entire ship would back you."

"Dangerous . . . dangerous," Fraffin said.

"But enough profit to oppose any danger," she said. "*Any* danger?"

"As the parable has it," Ynvic said, "the Gods smile on profit."

Gods, commerce and bureaucracy, Fraffin thought. *These endure, even among our poor savages. But I'm trapped here, grown too much like my simple creatures.* He held out his right hand, looked at the palm. *My hand's in their every heritage. I'm the germ of yesterday resurrecting faces out of Babylon.*

"Kelexel has requested an interview with the great Fraffin," Ynvic said. "He's been. . . ."

"I'll see him," Fraffin said. He hid his palm in a clenched fist. "Yes. Send him to me."

"No!" Ynvic said. "Refuse him, let your agents . . ."

"On what grounds? I've seen other rich merchants."

"Any grounds. Whim, an artist's impulse, pressure of work."

"I think I shall see him. Is he internally instrumented?"

"Of course not; they wouldn't be that simple. But why would you. . . ."

"To feel him out."

"You've professionals for that job."

"But he wants to see me."

"Here is real danger. Let him once suspect and he'll not bid. He'll just snoop until he has us all in his noose."

"He may not bid anyway. Someone must find what will tempt him."

"We *know* what'll tempt him! But let him get just the faintest hint that we can interbreed with these savages, the most vague suspicion and we've lost him . . . and ourselves as well."

"I'm not a child to be lectured to, Ynvic. I'll see him."

"You're determined, then?"

"I am. Where is he?"

"Out on the surface with a tour crew."

"Ahhh. And we're monitoring, of course. What does he think of our creatures?"

"The conventional things: they're so gross, ugly—, like caricatures of Chem humanity."

"But what do his eyes say?"

"The females interest him."

"Of course they do."

"Then you're going to withdraw from the war drama and set up a story for him?"

"What else can we do?" his voice revealed frustration and resignation.

"What'll you use, that little group in Delhi?"

"No, I'm saving that one for an emergency, a *real* emergency."

"The girls' school in Leeds?"

"Inappropriate. What do you think, Ynvic—will violence catch his mind?"

"Definitely. It's the murder school in Berlin, then, eh?"

"No, no! I think I have something much better. I'll discuss it after I've seen him. As soon as he returns, have . . ."

"One moment," Ynvic said. "Not the immune—not that one!"

"Why not? Compromise him completely."

"That's all this investigator would need! That alone without. . . ."

"The immune can be killed at any time," Fraffin said.

"This Kelexel is not stupid!"

"I'll be cautious."

"Just remember, old friend," Ynvic said, "that I'm in this as deeply as you. Most of the crew could probably get off with sentences of constructive labor, but I'm the one faked the gene samples we sent the Primacy."

"I heard you," Fraffin said. "The word is caution."

3

FEELING REASONABLY SECURE BEHIND HIS COVER,
Kelexel paused just inside the salon-office of the storyship director. He cast a searching look around the
room: such interesting signs of wear on furnishings
supposedly resistant to such depletion. The control
supports of an editing chair showed a polished glitter
where Fraffin's arms had rested.

He has been here a very long time indeed, Kelexel
thought. *We are right to suspect the worst. A Chem's
attention span cannot be that long—unless there are
forbidden attractions.*

"Visitor Kelexel," Fraffin said, rising. He indicated a
chair facing him across the desk, a simple wooden arti-
fact native to this place. It was a nice touch of the exotic, made a stranger feel uncomfortably alien and un-
adapted to outpost living. Fraffin himself occupied a
conventional floater seat, its body sensors tuned to his
personal needs.

Kelexel bowed over the immersed viewer in the
desk, used the formal greeting: "Director Fraffin, the
light of a billion suns could not add one candlepower
to thy brilliance."

Oh, Lords of Being, Fraffin thought. *One of those!*
He smiled, timed his seating to coincide with Kelexel.

"I grow dim in the presence of my guest," Fraffin
said. "How may I serve such a distinguished person?"
And he thought: *Preferably on buttered toast.*

Kelexel swallowed, felt suddenly uneasy. Something
about Fraffin bothered him. The director was such a
small man—dwarfed by the desk and its instruments.
Fraffin's skin was the milk-silver of the Sirihadi Chem,
almost matching the room's walls. It was the man's

stature; that was it. Kelexel had expected someone larger—not as large as the vassals of this planet, certainly ... but ... larger ... something to go with all the power visible in his features.

"You were very kind to grant me your time," Kelexel said.

Conventionally, Fraffin said: "What is time to the Chem?"

But Kelexel didn't rise to the cliche. The power in Fraffin's face! It was a famous face, of course—the black hair, the pits of eyes under jutting brows, crag cheeks, outcroppings of nose and jaw. Large reproductions of that face danced on the air wherever a Fraffin story was shown. But the actual flesh and bone man bore an unretouched resemblance to the reproductions that Kelexel found disturbing. He had expected more false drama in one or the other. He had expected disparity, a sham somewhere to help him see through these people.

"Visitors don't usually request an interview with the director," Fraffin said, prodding.

"Yes, yes, of course," Kelexel said. "I've a ..." He hesitated, realization coming over him. Everything about Fraffin—timbre of voice, the rich skin color, the total aura of vitality—it all spoke of recent rejuvenation. But Fraffin's cycle was known to the Bureau. He wasn't due for rejuvenation in this period.

"Yes?" Fraffin said.

"I've ... a rather personal request," Kelexel said.

"Not for employment, I hope," Fraffin said. "We've so ..."

"Nothing for myself," Kelexel said. "My interest level is quite low. Travel seems to satisfy me. However, during my last cycle I was permitted to have a male offspring."

"How fortunate for you," Fraffin said, and he held himself still and watchful, wondering: *Could the man know? Is it possible?*

"Mmmm, yes," Kelexel said. "My offspring, however, requires constant diversion. I'm prepared to pay a very high price for the privilege of placing him with your organization until my contract of responsibility terminates."

Kelexel sat back, waiting. *"He will be suspicious of you, naturally,"* the Bureau's experts had said. *"He will think you seek to place a spy among his crewmen. Be alert to his inner reactions when you make your offer."*

Watching now, Kelexel saw the Director's disquiet. *Is he fearful?* Kelexel wondered. *He shouldn't be fearful—not yet.*

"If saddens me," Fraffin said, "But no matter the offer, I must refuse."

Kelexel pursed his lips, then: "Would you refuse . . ." And he named a price that astonished Fraffin.

That's half as much as I could get for my entire planetary holding, Fraffin thought. *Is it possible Ynvic's wrong about him? This couldn't be an attempt to put a spy among us. All our crewmen are bound to the compact of shared guilt. No new man can learn what we do until he's hopelessly compromised. And the Bureau wouldn't try to buy one of us. They don't dare give me grounds for pleading entrapment.*

"Is it not enough?" Kelexel asked. He stroked his chin. The Bureau's experts had said: *"You must act the part of a responsible citizen concerned over his parental contract, perhaps even a bit doting and slightly embarrassed by it."*

"It, uhh, grieves me," Fraffin said, "but there's no price I'll accept. Were I to lower the barriers to one rich man's offspring, my ship soon would become a haven for dilettantes. We're a working crew, chosen only for talent. If your offspring wishes to train for a post, however, and go through the normal channels. . . ."

"Not even if I doubled the offer?" Kelexel asked.

Is it really the Bureau behind this clown? Fraffin wondered. *Or could he be one of the Galaxy Buyers?*

Fraffin cleared his throat. "No price. I *am* sorry."

"Perhaps I've offended you?"

"No. It's just that my decision is dictated by self-preservation. Work is our answer to the Chem nemesis. . . ."

"Ahh, boredom," Kelexel murmured.

"Precisely," Fraffin said. "Were I to open the doors to any bored person with enough wealth, I'd multiply all our problems. Just today I dismissed four crewmen for actions that'd be commonplace were I to hire my people the way you suggest."

"Four dismissed?" Kelexel said. "Lords of Preservation! What'd they do?"

"Deliberately lowered their shields, let the natives see them. Enough of that happens by accident without compounding it."

How honest and law abiding he tries to appear, Kelexel thought. *But the core of his crew has been with him too long, and those who leave—even the ones he dismisses—won't talk. Something's at work here which can't be explained by legality.*

"Yes, yes, of course," Kelexel said, assuming a slightly pompous air. "Can't have fraternizing with the natives out there." He gestured toward the surface with a thumb. "Illegal, naturally. Damnably dangerous."

"Raises the immunity level," Fraffin said.

"Must keep your execution squads busy."

Fraffin allowed himself a touch of pride, said: "I've had to send them after fewer than a million immunes on my planet. I let the natives kill their own."

"Only way," Kelexel agreed. "Keep us out of it as much as possible. Classic technique. You're justly famous for your success at it. Wanted my son to learn under you."

"I'm sorry," Fraffin said.

"Answer's definitely no?"

"Definitely."

Kelexel shrugged. The Bureau'd prepared him for outright rejection, but he hadn't quite prepared himself for it. He'd hoped to play out the little game of negotiation. "I hope I haven't offended you," he said.

"Of course not," Fraffin said. And he thought: *But you've warned me.*

He had come around to complete agreement with Ynvic's suspicions. It was something about this Kelexel's manner—an inward caution that didn't fit the outer mask.

"Glad of that," Kelexel said.

"I'm always curious about the merchant world's current price," Fraffin said. "I'm surprised you didn't bid on my entire holding."

You think I've made a mistake, Kelexel thought. *Fool! Criminals never learn.*

"My holdings are too diverse, require too much of my attention as it is," Kelexel said. "Naturally, I'd thought of bidding you out and giving all this to my offspring, but I'm quite certain he'd make a mess of it, ruin it for everyone. Couldn't invite that sort of censure on myself, you know."

"Perhaps the alternative, then," Fraffin said. "Training, the normal channels of application. . . ."

Kelexel had been prepared and sharpened for this task over a period long even to the Chem. The Primacy and the Bureau contained men who fed on suspicion and they smarted under continued failure with Fraffin's case. Now, the tiny betrayals in Fraffin's manner, the patterned evasions and choice of words were summed up in the Investigator's awareness. There was illegality here, but none of the crimes they'd considered and discussed. Somewhere in Fraffin's private domain there was a dangerous something—odorous and profoundly offensive. What could it be?

"If it is permitted," Kelexel said, "I shall be happy to study your operation and make appropriate suggestions to my offspring. He will be delighted, I know, to hear that the great Director Fraffin granted me these few attentions."

And Kelexel thought: *Whatever your crime is, I'll find it. When I do, you'll pay, Fraffin; you'll pay the same as any other malefactor.*

"Very well, then," Fraffin said. He expected Kelexel to leave now, but the man remained, staring offensively across the desk.

"One thing," Kelexel said. "I know you achieve quite complex special effects with your creatures. The extreme care, the precision engineering of motives and violence—I just wondered: Isn't it rather slow work?"

The casual ignorance of the question outraged Fraffin, but he sensed a warning in it and remembered Ynvic's words of caution.

"Slow?" he asked. "What's slow to people who deal with infinity?"

Ahh, Fraffin can be goaded, Kelexel thought as he read the signs of betrayal. *Good.* He said: "I merely wondered if . . . I hesitate to suggest it . . . but does not slowness equate with boredom?"

Fraffin sniffed. He'd thought at first this creature of the Bureau might be interesting, but the fellow was beginning to pall. Fraffin pressed a button beneath his desk, the signal to get the new story under way. The sooner they were rid of this investigator the better. All the preparations with the natives would help now. They'd play out their parts with rigorous nicety.

"I've offended you at last," Kelexel said, contrition in his voice.

"Have my stories bored you?" Fraffin asked. "If so, then I've offended you."

"Never!" Kelexel said. "So amusing, humorous. Such diversity."

Amusing, Fraffin thought. *Humorous!*

He glanced at the replay monitor in his desk, the strip of story action in progress, shielded and displayed there for only his eyes. His crews already were getting to work. The time was ripe for death. His people knew the urgency.

His mind went down, down—immersed in the desk viewer, forgetting the Investigator, following the petty lives of the natives.

They are the finite and we the infinite, Fraffin thought. *Paradox: the finite provides unlimited entertainment for the infinite. With such poor creatures we insulate ourselves from lives that are endless serial events. Aii, boredom! How you threaten the infinite.*

"How pliable your creatures are," Kelexel said, probing.

Such a bore, this clod, Fraffin thought. And he spoke without looking up from the viewer: "They've strong desires. I saw to that from the beginning And enormous fears—they have enormous fears."

"You saw to that, too?" Kelexel asked.

"Naturally!"

How easily he's goaded to anger, Kelexel thought.

"What is that you're watching?" Kelexel asked. "Is it something to do with a story? Do I interfere?"

He begins to take the hook, Fraffin thought. And he said: "I've just started a new story, a little gem."

"A new story?" Kelexel asked, puzzled. "Is the war epic completed then?"

"I've cut off that story," Fraffin said. "It wasn't going well at all. Besides, wars are beginning to bore me. But personal conflict now—there's the thing!"

"*Personal* conflict?" Kelexel felt the idea was appalling.

"Ah, the intimacies of violence," Fraffin said. "Anyone can find drama in wars and migrations, in the rise and fall of civilizations and of religions—but what would you think of a little capsule of a story that focuses on a creature who slays its mate?"

Kelexel shook his head. The conversation had taken a turn that left him floundering. The war epic abandoned? A new story? Why? His forebodings returned. Was there a way Fraffin could harm a fellow Chem?

"Conflict and fear," Fraffin said. "Ahh, what a wide avenue into the susceptibilities these are."

"Yes . . . yes, indeed," Kelexel murmured.

"I touch a nerve," Fraffin said. "Greed here, a desire there, a whim in this place—and fear. Yes, fear. When the creature's fully prepared, I arouse its fears. Then the whole mechanism performs for me. They make themselves ill! They love! They hate! They cheat! They kill! They die."

Fraffin smiled—clenched teeth in the wide mouth. Kelexel found the expression menacing.

"And the most amusing part," Fraffin said, "the most *humorous* element is that they think they do it of and by themselves."

Kelexel forced an answering smile. Many times he'd laughed at this device in a Fraffin story, but now he found the idea less than amusing. He swallowed, said: "But wouldn't such a story . . ." He groped for the proper expression. ". . . be so . . . small?"

Small, Fraffin thought. *Such a clown, this Kelexel.*

"Is it not an ultimate artistry," Fraffin asked, "if I use a microscopic incident to display immensity? I take the Forever-Now right here." He lifted a clenched fist, extended it toward Kelexel, opened it to show the palm. "I give you something you don't have—mortality."

Kelexel found the thought repellant—Fraffin and his grubby personal conflict, a slaying, a petty crime. What a depressing idea. But Fraffin was absorbed once more in the shielded viewer on his desk. What did he see there?

"I fear I've overstayed my welcome," Kelexel ventured.

Fraffin jerked his gaze upward. The clod was going. Good. He wouldn't go far. The net already was being prepared. What a fine, entangling mesh it had!

"The freedom of the ship is yours," Fraffin said.

"Forgive me if I've taken too much of your time," Kelexel said, rising.

Fraffin stood, bowed, made the conventional response: "What is time to the Chem?"

Kelexel murmured the formal reply: "Time is our toy." He turned, strode from the room, thoughts whirling in his mind. There was menace in Fraffin's manner. It had something to do with what he saw in that viewer. A story? How could a story menace a Chem?

Fraffin watched the door seal itself behind Kelexel, sank back into his chair and returned his attention to the viewer. It was night up there on the surface now and the crucial first incident was beginning to unfold.

A native killing its mate. He watched, and struggled to maintain his artistic distance. Subject female, appellation Murphey, a figure of staggering scarlet under artificial lights. The fog of all pretense scorched from her features by the unexpected alien who had been her husband. She submitted her life now to formidable auguries of which she'd had not the slightest hint. The weirds and shades of her ancestral gods no longer awakened mysteries in her mind. The doomfire faces of superstition had lost their accustomed places.

With an abrupt, violent motion, Fraffin blanked out the viewer, put his hands to his face. Death had come to the creature. The story would go on of itself now, under its own momentum. What a way to trap a Chem!

Fraffin lowered his hands to the smooth cold surface of his desk. But who was trapped?

He felt himself stretched suddenly upon a rack of vision, sensed a frightened multitude within him—the whisperings of his own past without beginning.

What were we—once? he wondered.

There lay the Chem curse: the infinite possessed no antiquities. Memory blurred off back there and one went to the artificial memory of records and reels with all their inaccuracies.

What was lost there? he wondered. *Did we have damned prophets with the sickness of butchery on their tongues, their words casting out the salt of fate? What spiced fantasy might we uncover in our lost beginnings? We've gods of our own making. How did we make them? Do we spit now upon our own dust as we laugh at my foolish, pliable natives?*

He could not deflect the sudden swarming of his own past—like hungry beasts glowing in a sky he'd beheld only once but which had terrorized him into flight. As quickly as it had come, the fear dissipated. But the experience left him shaken. He stared at one of his own hands. The hand trembled.

I need distracting entertainment, he thought. *Gods of Preservation! Even boredom's preferable to this!*

Fraffin pushed himself away from his desk. How cold its edge felt against his hands! The room had become a foreign place, its devices alien, hateful. The soft curves of his massage couch, still shaped to his body, caught his attention on the right and he looked away quickly, repelled by his own body's outline.

I must do something rational, he thought.

With a determined effort, he stood, made his way across the room to the steely convolutions of his pantovive reproducer. He slumped into its padded control seat, tuned the sensors directly to the planet surface. Satellite relays locked onto the machine's probes and he searched out the daylight hemisphere, looked for activity there among his creatures—anything in which to bury his awareness.

Land swam through the viewer stage, a wash of checkerboard outlines in greens and yellows with here and there a chocolate brown. Highways . . . roads . . . the glittering amoeba shape of the city—he focused down into the streets and abruptly had a small crowd centered on the stage, the quarter-sized figures huddled like dolls at a corner. They were watching a pitchman, a weasel-faced little giant in a wrinkled gray suit and greasy hat. The native stood covertly alert behind a flimsy stand tray with transparent cover.

"Fleas!" the pitchman said and his voice carried that intimate imperative of the natural confidence man. "Yes, that's what they are: fleas. But through an ancient and secret training method I make them perform fantastic acrobatics and marvelous tricks for you. See this pretty girl dance. And there's a little woman who pulls a chariot. And this little girl leaps hurdles! They'll wrestle and race and romp for you! Step right up. Only one lira to look through the magnifying viewers and see these marvels!"

Do those Fleas know they're someone's property? Fraffin wondered.

4

FOR DR. ANDROCLES THURLOW, IT BEGAN WITH A telephone ringing in the night.

Thurlow's fumbling hand knocked the receiver to the floor. He spent a moment groping for it in the dark, still half asleep. His mind held trailing bits of a dream in which he relived the vivid moments just before the blast at the Lawrence Radiation lab which had injured his eyes. It was a familiar dream that had begun shortly after the accident three months ago, but he felt that it now contained a new significance which he'd have to examine professionally.

Psychologist, heal thyself, he thought.

The receiver gave off a tinny voice which helped him locate it. He pressed it to his ear.

"Hullo." His voice carried a rasping sound in a dry mouth.

"Andy?"

He cleared his throat. "Yes?"

"This is Clint Mossman."

Thurlow sat up, swung his feet out of the bed. The rug felt cold against his soles. The luminous dial of his bedside clock showed 2:18 A.M. The time and the fact that Mossman was the County's chief criminal deputy sheriff could only mean an emergency. Mossman wanted *Dr.* Thurlow in his capacity as court psychologist.

"You there, Andy?"

"I'm here, Clint. What is it?"

"I'm afraid I have bad news, Andy. Your old girl friend's daddy just killed her mother."

For a moment, the words made no sense. *Old girl*

friend. He had only one old girl friend here, but she was now married to someone else.

"It's Joe Murphey, Ruth Hudson's daddy," Mossman said.

"Oh, God," Thurlow muttered.

"I haven't much time," Mossman said. "I'm calling from a pay phone across the street from Joe's office building. He's holed up in his office and he has a gun. He says he'll only surrender to you."

Thurlow shook his head. "He wants to see me?"

"We need you down here right away, Andy. I know this is a tough one for you—Ruth and all, but I've no choice. I want to prevent a gun battle. . . ."

"I warned you people something like this was going to happen," Thurlow said. He felt a sudden angry resentment against Mossman, the entire community of Moreno.

"I haven't time to argue with you," Mossman said. "I've told him you're coming. It shouldn't take more'n twenty minutes to get down here. Hurry it up, will you?"

"Sure, Clint. Right away."

Thurlow put the receiver back on the phone. He prepared himself for the pain of light, turned on the bedside lamp. His eyes began to water immediately. He blinked rapidly, wondered if he'd ever again be able to experience sudden light without pain.

The realization of what Mossman had said began to grow. His mind felt numb. *Ruth! Where is Ruth?* But that wasn't his concern any more. That was Nev Hudson's problem. He began dressing, moving softly as he'd learned to do in the nights when his father was still alive.

He took his wallet from the night stand, found his wristwatch and buckled it onto his left wrist. The glasses, then—the special polarizing glasses with their adjustable lenses. His eyes relaxed as soon as he put them on. The light took on a sharply defined yellow cast. He looked up, caught a view of himself in the mirror: thin face, the dark glasses behind heavy black rims, black crewcut hair high at the temples, nose long with a slight bulge below the glasses, wide mouth with slightly thicker lower lip, Lincolnesque chin, blue-shadowed and with divergent scar-like creases.

A drink was what he needed, but he knew he couldn't take the time. *Poor, sick Joe Murphey*, he thought. *God what a mess!*

5

THURLOW COUNTED FIVE SHERIFF'S CARS DRAWN UP
at an angle to the curb in front of the Murphey Building as he pulled to a stop across the street. Spotlights
drew patterns of erratic brilliance across the front of
the three-story building and the blue and white sign
above the entrance: "J.H. MURPHEY COMPANY—
FINE COSMETICS."

The lights reflected bursts of brilliance off the sign.
The reflections speared Thurlow's eyes. He slipped out
on the curbside, searched for Mossman. Two furtive
huddles of men crouched behind cars across the street.

Has Joe been shooting at them? Thurlow wondered.

He knew he was exposed to the dark windows of the
building across there, but he felt none of the fragile
loneliness he'd experienced in fire fights across the rice
paddies of the war. He felt it was impossible that
Ruth's father could shoot at him. There'd been only
one direction for the man to explode—and he'd already done that. Murphey was used up now, little more
than a shell.

One of the officers across the street pushed a bull-
horn around the rear of a car, shouted into it: "Joe!
You, Joe Murphey! Dr. Thurlow's here. Now you
come down out of there and give yourself up. We don't
want to have to come in there shooting."

The amplified voice boomed and echoed between the
buildings. In spite of the amplifier's distortions, Thurlow recognized Mossman's voice.

A second floor window of the Murphey Building
opened with a chilling screech. Spotlight circles darted
across the stone facing, centered the movement. A
man's voice shouted from darkness behind the win-

25

dow: "No need to get rough, Clint, I see him over there. I'll be down in seven minutes." The window banged shut.

Thurlow ducked around his car, ran across to Mossman. The deputy was a bone thin man in a sack-like tan suit and pale cream sombrero. He turned to reveal a narrow face full of craggy shadows from the spotlights' reflections.

"Hi, Andy," he said. "Sorry about this, but you see how it is."

"Has he been shooting?" Thurlow asked. He was surprised at the calmness of his own voice. *Professional training*, he thought. This was a psychotic crisis and he was trained to handle such matters.

"No, but he's got a gun all right," Mossman said. The deputy's voice sounded weary and disgusted.

"You plan to give him his seven minutes?"

"Should we?"

"I think so. I think he'll do exactly what he said he'll do. He'll come down and give himself up."

"Seven minutes and no more then."

"Did he say why he wanted to see me?"

"Something about Ruth and he's afraid we'll shoot him if you're not here."

"Is that what he said?"

"Yeah."

"He's living in a rather involved fantasy, that's clear," Thurlow said. "Perhaps I should go up and...."

"I'm afraid I can't risk giving him a hostage."

Thurlow sighed.

"You're here," Mossman said. That's what he asked for. I'll go along with...."

A radio speaker in the car beside them emitted a clanging sound, then: "Car nine."

Mossman leaned into the car, put the microphone to his mouth, thumbed the button: "This is car nine, over."

Thurlow looked around, recognized some of the officers sheltered behind the cars. He nodded to the ones who met his gaze, finding it odd how familiar and yet unfamiliar the men appeared, their faces dim in the polarized light which his lenses admitted. They were men he saw frequently in the courthouse, men he knew by first name, but now they exposed a side he'd never before seen.

A metallic crackling came from Mossman's radio, then: "Jack wants to know your ten-oh-eight, car nine. Over."

Has Ruth heard yet? Thurlow wondered. *Who'll break this to her . . . and how?*

"Murphey's still up there in his office," Mossman said. "Dr. Thurlow's here now and Murphey says he'll give himself up in seven minutes. We're going to wait him out. Over."

"Okay, car nine. Jack's on his way with four more men. Sheriff's still out at the house with the coroner. Sheriff says don't take any chances. Use gas if you have to. Time is two forty-six; over."

"Car nine is seven-oh-five," Mossman said. "Over and out." He hung the microphone in its rack, turned back to Thurlow. "What a sweet mess!" He pushed his cream sombrero back from his forehead.

"There's no doubt he killed Adele?" Thurlow asked.

"No doubt."

"Where?"

"At their house."

"How?"

"Knife—that big souvenir thing he was always waving around at barbecues."

Thurlow took a deep breath. It fitted the pattern, of course. A knife was the sickly logical weapon. He forced himself to professional calmness, asked: "When?"

"About midnight near as we can figure. Somebody called an ambulance but they didn't think to notify us for almost half an hour. By the time we got on it Joe was gone."

"So you came down here looking for him?"

"Something like that."

Thurlow shook his head. As he moved, one of the spotlights shifted and he thought he saw an object hanging in the air outside Murphey's window. He jerked his attention upward and the object appeared to flow backward up into the dark sky. Thurlow removed his glasses, rubbed his eyes. Strange thing—it had looked like a long tube. An aftereffect from the injury to his eyes, he thought. He replaced the glasses, returned his attention to Mossman.

"What's Joe doing in there?" Thurlow asked. "Any idea?"

"Calling people on the telephone, bragging about what he's done. His secretary, Nella Hartnick, had to be taken to the hospital in hysterics."

"Has he called . . . Ruth?"

"Dunno."

Thurlow thought about Ruth then, really focused on her for the first time since she'd sent back his ring with the polite little note (so unlike her, that note) telling of her marriage to Nev Hudson. Thurlow had been in Denver on the fellowship grant that had come to him through the National Science Foundation.

What a fool I was, he thought. *That grant wasn't worth losing Ruth.*

He wondered if he should call her, try to break this news to her as gently as possible. But he knew there was no gentle way to break this news. It had to be done swiftly, cruel and sharp. A clean wound that would heal with as small a scar as possible . . . under the circumstances.

Moreno being the small town it was, he knew Ruth had kept her job after her marriage—night shift psychiatric nurse at the County Hospital. She'd be at the hospital now. A telephone call would be too impersonal, he knew. It'd have to be done in person.

And I'd be irrevocably associated with the tragedy, he thought. *I don't want that.*

Thurlow realized then that he was daydreaming, trying to hold onto something of what he and Ruth had known together. He sighed. Let someone else break the news to her. She was someone else's responsibility now.

An officer on Thurlow's right said: "Think he's drunk?"

"Is he ever sober?" Mossman asked.

The first officer asked: "You see the body?"

"No," Mossman said, "but Jack described it when he called me."

"Just gi'me one good shot at the sonofabitch," the first officer muttered.

And now it starts, Thurlow thought.

He turned as a car pulled to a screeching stop across the street. Out of it jumped a short fat man, his pants pulled over pajamas. The man carried a camera with strobe light.

Thurlow whirled away from the light as the man crouched and aimed the camera. The strobe light flared in the canyon of the street . . . and again.

Expecting the glare, Thurlow had looked up at the sky to avoid the reflected light and its pain on his injured eyes. As the strobe flashed, he saw the strange object once more. It was hanging in the air about ten feet out from Murphey's window. Even after the flare of light, the thing remained visible as a dim shape, almost cloudlike.

Thurlow stared, entranced. This couldn't be an illusion or aftereffect of the eye injury. The shape was quite definite, real. It appeared to be a cylinder about twenty feet long and four or five feet in diameter. A semicircular shelf like a Ubangi lip projected from the end nearest the building. Two figures crouched on the lip. They appeared to be aiming a small stand-mounted tube at Murphey's window. The figures were indistinct in the fog-like outline, but they appeared human—two arms, two legs—although small: perhaps only three feet tall.

Thurlow felt an odd sense of detached excitement at the vision. He knew he was seeing something real whose strangeness defied explanation. As he stared, one of the figures turned, looked full at him. Thurlow saw the glow of eyes through the cloud-blurring. The figure nudged its companion. Now, both of them peered down at Thurlow—two pairs of glowing eyes.

Is it some form of mirage? he wondered.

Thurlow tried to swallow in a dry throat. A mirage could be seen by anyone. Mossman, standing beside him, was staring up at Murphey's window. The deputy couldn't help but see that odd cylinder hovering there—or the vision of it—but he gave no sign.

The photographer came panting up to them. Thurlow knew the man: Tom Lee from the *Sentinel*.

"Is Murphey still in there?" Lee asked.

"That's right," Mossman said.

"Hi, Dr. Thurlow," Lee said. "What you staring at? Is that the window where Murphey's holed up?"

Thurlow grabbed Lee's shoulder. The two creatures on the cylinder had returned to their tube and were aiming it down toward the crowd of officers. Thurlow pointed toward them, aware of a strong musky smell of cologne from the photographer.

"Tom, what the devil is that up there?" Thurlow asked. "Get a picture of it."

Lee turned with his camera, looked up. "What? Picture of what?"

"That thing outside Murphey's window."

"What thing?"

"Don't you see something hovering just out from that window?"

"A bunch of gnats, maybe. Lots of 'em this year. They always collect like that where there's light."

"What light?" Thurlow asked.

"Huh? Well. . . ."

Thurlow yanked off his polarized glasses. The cloud-like cylinder disappeared. In its place was a vague, foggy shape with tiny movements in it. He could see the corner of the building through it. He replaced the glasses. Again, there was a cylinder with two figures on a lip projecting from it. The figures were now pointing their tube toward the building's entrance.

"There he comes!" It was a shout from their left.

Lee almost knocked Thurlow down pushing past Mossman to aim the camera at the building's entrance. Officers surged forward.

Thurlow stood momentarily alone as a short, stocky, partly bald man in a blue suit appeared in the spotlight glare at the street doors of the Murphey Building. The man threw one hand across his eyes as the spotlights centered on him and the strobe light flared. Thurlow blinked in the glare of light. His eyes watered.

Deputies engulfed the man at the doors.

Lee darted off to one side, lifted the camera over-head, pointing it down at the milling group. "Let me see his face!" Lee called. "Open up there a little."

But the officers ignored him.

Again, the strobe flared.

Thurlow had one more glimpse of the captive—small eyes blinking in a round florid face. How curi-ously intense the eyes—unafraid. They stared out at the psychologist, recognizing him.

"Andy!" Murphey shouted. "Take care of Ruthy! You hear? Take care of Ruthy!"

Murphey became a jerking bald spot hustled along in a crowd of hats. He was pushed into a car off near the corner on the right. Lee still hovered on the out-skirts firing his strobe light.

Thurlow took a shuddering breath. There was a sense of charged air around him, a pack smell mingled with exhaust gasses as the cars were started. Belatedly, he remembered the cylinder at the window, looked up in time to see it lift away from the building, fade into the sky.

There was a nightmare feeling to the vision, the noise, the shouted orders around him.

A deputy paused beside Thurlow, said: "Clint says thanks. He says you can talk to Joe in a coupla hours—after the D.A. gets through with him, or in the morning if you'd rather."

Thurlow wet his lips with his tongue, tasted acid in his throat. He said: "I . . . in the morning, I think. I'll check the probation department for an appointment."

"Isn't going to be much pretrial nonsense about this case," the deputy said. "I'll tell Clint what you said." He got into the car beside Thurlow.

Lee came up, the camera now on a strap around his neck. He held a notebook in his left hand, a stub pencil in his right.

"Hey, Doc," he said, "is that right what Mossman said? Murphey wouldn't come out until you got here?"

Thurlow nodded, stepped aside as the patrol car backed out. The question sounded completely inane, something born of the same kind of insanity that left him standing here in the street as cars sped off around the corner in a wake of motor sounds. The smell of unburned gas was sharp and stinging in his nostrils.

Lee scribbled in the notebook.

"Weren't you pretty friendly with Murphey's daughter once?" Lee asked.

"We're friends," Thurlow said. The mouth that spoke the words seemed to belong to someone else.

"You see the body?" Lee asked.

Thurlow shook his head.

"What a sweet, bloody mess," Lee said.

Thurlow wanted to say: *"You're a sweet, bloody pig!"* but his voice wouldn't obey him. Adele Murphey . . . a body. Bodies in crimes of violence tended toward an ugly sameness: the sprawl, the red wetness, the dark wounds . . . the professional detachment of police as they recorded and measured and questioned. Thurlow could feel his own professional detachment deserting him. This body that Lee mentioned with such avid concern for the story, this body was a person Thurlow had known—mother of the woman he'd loved . . . still loved.

Thurlow admitted this to himself now, remembering Adele Murphey, the calmly amused looks from eyes so like Ruth's . . . and the measuring stares that said she wondered what kind of husband he'd make for her daughter. But that was dead, too. That had died first.

"Doc, what was it you thought you saw up by that window?" Lee asked.

Thurlow looked down at the fat little man, the thick lips, the probing, wise little eyes, and thought what the reaction would be to a description of that *thing* hovering outside Murphey's window. Involuntarily, Thurlow glanced up at the window. The space was empty now. The night had grown suddenly cold. Thurlow shivered.

"Was Murphey looking out?" Lee asked.

The man's voice carried an irritating country twang that rasped on Thurlow's nerves.

"No," Thurlow said. "I . . . I guess I just saw a reflection.

"I don't know how you can see anything through those glasses," Lee said.

"You're right," Thurlow said. "It was the glasses, my eyes—a reflection."

"I've a lot more questions, Doc," Lee said. "You wanta stop up at the Turk's Nightery where we can be comfortable. We can go in my car and I'll bring. . . ."

"No," Thurlow said. He shook his head, feeling the numbness pass. "No. Maybe tomorrow."

"Hell, Doc, it *is* tomorrow."

But Thurlow turned away, ran across the street to his car. His mind had come fully to focus on Murphey's words: *"Take care of Ruthy."*

Thurlow knew he had to find Ruth, offer any help he could. She was married to someone else, but that didn't end what had been between them.

6

THE AUDIENNCE STIRRED, A SINGLE ORGANISM IN THE anonymous darkness of the storyship's empatheater.

Kelexel, seated near the center of the giant room, felt that oddly menacing dark movement. They were all around him, the story cadre and off-duty crewmen interested in Fraffin's new production. They had seen two reels run and rerun a dozen times while the elements were refined. They waited now for another rerun of the opening scene, and still Kelexel sensed that threatening aura in this place. It was personal and direct, something to do with the *story*, but he couldn't define it.

He could smell now the faint bite of ozone from the sensimesh web, that offshoot from Tiggywaugh's discovery, whose invisible field linked the audience to the story projection. His chair felt strange. It was professional equipment with solid arms and keyed flanges for the editing record. Only the vast domed ceiling with its threads of pantovive force focusing down, down onto the stage far below him (and the stage itself)—these were familiar, like any normal empatheater.

But the sounds, the clicks of editing keys, professional comments—"Shorten that establishment and get to the closeup. . . ." "Hit the olfactory harder as soon as you have light. . . ." "Soften that first breeze effect. . . ." "Amplify the victim's opening emotion and cut back immediately. . . ."

All this continued to be discord.

Kelexel had spent two working days in here, privileged to watch the cadre at its chores. Still, the sounds and voices of the audience remained discord. His previous experience of empatheaters had always involved completed stories and rapt watchers.

34

Far off to his left in the darkness, a voice said: "Roll it."

The pantovive force lines disappeared. Utter blackness filled the room.

Someone cleared his throat. Clearing throats became a message of nervousness that wove out through the dark.

Light came into being at the center of the stage. Kelexel squirmed into a more comfortable position. Always, that same old beginning, he thought. The light was a forlorn, formless thing that resolved slowly into a streetlamp. It illuminated a slope of lawn, a curved length of driveway and in the background the ghost-gray wall of a native house. The dark windows of primitive glass glistened like strange eyes.

There was a panting noise somewhere in the scene and something thudding with a frenzied rhythm.

An insect chirred.

Kelexel felt the realism of the sounds as pantovive circuits reproduced them with all the values of the original. To sit enmeshed in the web, linked to the empathic projectors, was as real as viewing the original raw scene from a vantage point above and to one side. It was, in its own way, like the Chem oneness. The smell of dust from wind-stirred dry grass permeated Kelexel's awareness. A cool finger of breeze touched his face.

Terror crept through Kelexel then. It reached out from the shadowy scene and through the web's projectors with a billowing insistence. Kelexel had to remind himself that this was story artistry, that it wasn't real . . . for him. He was experiencing another creature's fear caught and preserved on sensitive recorders.

A running figure, a native woman clad in a loose green gown that billowed around her thighs, fled into the focus on the stage. She gasped and panted as she ran. Her bare feet thudded on the lawn and then on the paving of the driveway. Pursuing her came a squat, moon-faced man carrying a sword whose blade like a silvery snaketrack glittered in the light of the streetlamp.

Terror radiated from the woman. She gasped: "No! Please, dear God, no!"

Kelexel held his breath. No matter the number of times he had seen this, the act of violence felt new each time. He was beginning to see what Fraffin might have in this story. The sword was lifted high overhead. . . .

"Cut!"

The web went blank, no emotion, nothing. It was like being dropped off a cliff. The stage darkened.

Kelexel realized then the voice had been Fraffin's. It had come from far down to the right. A momentary rage at Fraffin's action surged through Kelexel. It required a moment for the Investigator to reorient himself and still he felt frustrated.

Lights came on revealing the rising wedge of seats converging on the disc of stage. Kelexel blinked, stared around him at the story cadre. He could still feel the menace from them and from that empty stage. What was the threat here? he wondered. He trusted his instincts in this: there was danger in this room. But *what* was it?

The cadre sat around him row on row—trainees and off-duty crewmen at the rear, probationers and specialist observers in the center, the editing crew down near the stage. Taken individually, they appeared such ordinary Chem, but Kelexel remembered what he had felt in the dark—the oneness, an organism bent on harming him, *confident* of its ability to harm him. He could sense it in the Chem empathy, the all-one-life they shared.

There was an old stillness to the room now. They were waiting for something. Far down near the stage heads bent together in inaudible conversation.

Am I imagining things? Kelexel wondered. *But surely they must suspect me. Why then do they permit me to sit in here and watch them work?*

The work—that violent death.

Again, Kelexel felt frustration at the way Fraffin had cut off that scene. To have the vision denied him even when he knew how it went. . . . Kelexel shook his head. He felt confused, excited. Once more he swept his gaze over the cadre. They were a gaming board of colors in the giant room, the hue of each uniform coded to its wearer's duties—red patches of flitter pilots, the motley orange and black of shooting crewmen, green of story continuity, yellow of servicing and repair, purple of acting and white of wordrobe, and here and there the black punctuation marks of Manipulators, subdirectors. Fraffin's inner circle.

The group near the stage broke apart. Fraffin emerged, climbed up onto the stage and to the very center, the bare circle of image focus. It was a deliberate move which identified him with the action which had occupied that space only moments before.

Kelexel bent forward to study the Director. Fraffin was a gaunt little figure down there in his black cloak, a patch of ebony hair above silver skin, the gashed straightedge mouth with its deep upper lip. He was suddenly something from the shadowy marches of a far and perilous realm that no other Chem had ever glimpsed. There was an arresting individuality to him.

The sunken eyes looked up and searched out Kelexel.

A chill went through the Investigator then. He sat back, his thoughts boiling with alarm. It was as though Fraffin had spoken to him, saying: *"There's the foolish Investigator! There he is, ensnared in my net, trapped! Safely caught! Oh, certainly caught!"*

Silence gripped the empatheater now like a held breath. The intent faces of the cadre focused on the image stage.

"I will tell you once more," Fraffin said, and his vocie caressed the air. "Our aim is subtlety."

Again, Fraffin looked up at Kelexel.

Now, he has felt terror, Fraffin thought. *Fear heightens the sex drive. And he has seen the victim's daughter, a female of the kind to snare any Chem—exotic, not too gross, graceful, eyes like strange green jewels. Ah, how the Chem love green. She is sufficiently similiar to other non-Chem pleasure creatures that he will sense new physical excitements in her. Ah, hah, Kelexel! You will ask to examine a native soon—and we'll permit it.*

"You are not keeping the viewer sufficiently in mind," Fraffin said. His voice had turned suddenly cold.

A shiver of agitation swept up through the empatheater.

"We must not make our viewer feel too deep a terror," Fraffin said. "Only let him know terror is present. Don't force the experience. Let him enjoy it—amusing violence, humorous death. The viewer must not think *he* is the one being manipulated. There is more here than a pattern of intrigue for our own enjoyment."

Kelexel sensed unspoken messages in Fraffin's words. A definite threat, yes. He felt the play of emotions around him and wondered at them.

I must get one of these natives to examine intimately and at my leisure, Kelexel thought. *Perhaps there's a clue that only a native can reveal.*

As though this thought were a key to the locked door of temptation, Kelexel found his mind suddenly filled with thoughts about a female from Fraffin's story. The name, such an exotic sound—Ruth. Red-haired Ruth. There was something of the Subicreatures about her and the Subi were famous for the erotic pleasures they gave the Chem. Kelexel remembered a Subi he had owned once. She had seemed to fade so rapidly, though. Mortals had a way of doing that when paced by the endless life of a Chem.

Perhaps I could examine this Ruth, Kelexel thought. *It'd be a simple matter for Fraffin's men to bring her to me here.*

"Subtlety," Fraffin said. "The audience must be maintained in a detached awareness. Think of our story as a form of dance, not real in the way *our* lives are real, but an interesting reflection, a Chem fairy story. By now, you all must know the purpose of our story. See that you hew to that purpose with proper subtlety."

Fraffin drew his black cloak around him with a feeling of amusement at the showmanship of the gesture. He turned his back on the audience, stalked off the stage.

It was a good crew, Fraffin reminded himself. They

would play their parts with trained exactitude. This amusing little story would accumulate on the reels. It might even be salable as an interlude piece, a demonstration of artistic deftness. But no matter; it would serve its purpose if it did no more than lead Kelexel around—a fear here, a desire there—his every move recorded by the shooting crews. Every move.

He's as easy to manipulate as the natives, Fraffin thought.

He let himself out through the service tube at the rear of the stage, emerged into the blue walls of the drop hall that curved down past the storage bays to his quarters. Fraffin allowed the drop field to catch him and propel him past the seamless projections of hatchways in a gentle blur.

It's almost possible to feel sorry for Kelexel, he thought.

The man had been so obviously repelled at first confrontation with the idea of single violence, but oh, how he'd lost himself in the native conflict when shown it.

We identify with individual acts of violence so easily, Fraffin thought. *One might almost suspect there were real experiences of this kind in our own pasts.*

He felt the reflexive tightening of the armor that was his skin, a sudden turmoil of unfixed memories. Fraffin swallowed, halted the drop at the hatchway outside his salon.

The endlessness of his own personal *story* appalled him suddenly. He felt that he stood on the brink of terrifying discoveries. He sensed monsters of awareness lurking in the shadows of eternity directly before him. *Things* loomed there which he dared not identify.

A pleading rage suffused Fraffin then. He wanted to slam a fist into eternity, to still the hidden voices gibbering at him. He felt himself go still with fear and he thought: *To be immortal is to require frequent administrations of moral anesthesia.*

It was such an odd thought that it dispelled his fear. He let himself into the silvery warmth of his salon wondering whence that thought had come.

7

THURLOW SAT SMOKING HIS PIPE, HUNCHED OVER THE wheel of his parked car. His polarizing glasses lay on the seat beside him, and he stared at the evening sky through raindrops luminous on the windshield. His eyes watered and the raindrops blurred like tears. The car was a five-year-old coupe and he knew he needed a new one, but he'd fallen into the habit of saving his money to buy a house . . . when he'd thought of marrying Ruth. The habit was difficult to break now, although he knew he clung to it mostly out of perverse hope that the past year might yet be erased from their lives.

Why does she want to see me? he wondered. *And why here, where we used to meet? Why such secrecy now?*

It had been two days since the murder and he found he still couldn't assemble the events of the period into a coherent whole. Where news stories mentioned his own involvement, those stories read like something written about a stranger—their meaning as blurred as the raindrops in front of him now. Thurlow felt his whole world invaded by Joe Murphey's psychotic ramblings and the violent reactions of the community.

It shocked Thurlow to realize that the community wanted Murphey dead. Public reaction had struck him with all the violence of the storm which had just passed.

Violent storm, he thought. *A violence storm.*

He looked up at the trees on his left, wondering how long he'd been here. His watch had stopped, unwound. Ruth was late, though. It was her way.

There'd been the storm. Clouds had grown out of a

hard gray sky with rain crouched low in them. For a time the eucalyptus grove around him had been filled with frightened bird sounds. A wind had hummed through the high boughs—then the rain: big spattering drops.

The sun was back now, low in the west, casting orange light onto the treetops. The leaves drooped with hanging raindrops. A mist near the ground quested among scaly brown trunks. Insect cries came from the roots and the bunchgrass that grew in open places along the dirt road into the grove.

What do they remember of their storm? Thurlow wondered.

He knew professionally why the community wanted its legal lynching, but to see the same attitude in officials, this was the shocker. Thurlow thought about the delays being placed in his path, the attempts to prevent his own professional examination of Murphey. The sheriff, district attorney George Paret, all the authorities knew by now that Thurlow had predicted the psychotic break which had cost Adele Murphey her life. If they recognized this as a fact, Murphey had to be judged insane and couldn't be executed.

Paret already had shown his hand by calling in Thurlow's own department chief, the Moreno State Hospital director of psychiatry, Dr. LeRoi Whelye. Whelye was known throughout the state as a hanging psychiatrist, a man who always found what the prosecution wanted. Right on schedule, Whelye had declared Murphey to be sane and "responsible for his acts."

Thurlow looked at his useless wristwatch. It was stopped at 2:14. He knew it must be closer to seven now. It would be dark soon. What was keeping Ruth? Why had she asked him to meet her in their old trysting place?

He felt suddenly contaminated by this way of meeting.

Am I ashamed to see her openly now? he asked himself.

Thurlow had come directly from the hospital and Whelye's unsubtle attempts to get him to step aside from this case, to forget for the moment that he was also the county's court psychologist.

The words had been direct: ". . . personal involvement . . . your old girl friend . . . her father. . . ." The meaning was clear, but underneath lay the awareness that Whelye, too, knew about that report on Murphey which rested now in the Probation Department's files. And that report contradicted Whelye's public stand.

Whelye had come up just as they were about to go into a Ward Team conference to consider the possible discharge of a patient. Thurlow thought of that conference now, sensing how it encapsulated the chief of psychiatry.

They'd been in the ward office with its smell of oiled floors and disinfectant—the Protestant chaplain, a small sandy-haired man whose dark suits always seemed too large and made him appear even smaller; the ward nurse, Mrs. Norman, heavy, gray-haired, busty, a drill sergeant's rocky face with cap always set squarely on her head; Dr. Whelye, an impression of excess bulk in a tweed suit, iron gray at the temples and in patches through his black hair, a sanitary and barber-scraped appearance to his pink cheeks, and a look of calculated reserve in his washed blue eyes.

Lastly, almost something to overlook around the scarred oval table, there'd been a patient: a number and a first name, Peter. He was seventeen, mentally limited by lack of the right genes, lack of opportunity, lack of education, lack of proper nutrition. He was a walking *lack*, blonde hair slicked down, veiled blue eyes, a narrow nose and pointed chin, a pursed-up little mouth, as though everything about him had to be shelled up inside and guarded.

Outside the room had been green lawns, sunshine and patients preparing the flower beds for Spring. Inside, Thurlow felt, there had been little more than the patient's smell of fear with Whelye conducting the interview like a district attorney.

"What kind of work are you going to do when you get out?" Whelye asked.

Peter, keeping his eyes on the table—"Sell newspapers or shine shoes, something like that."

"Can't make any money like that unless you have a big corner stand and then you're in big business," Whelye said.

Watching this, Thurlow wondered why the psychiatrist would suppress ideas instead of trying to draw the boy out. He asked himself then what Whelye would do if he, Thurlow, should stop the proceedings and take the patient's place to describe ". . . a thing I saw the other night, something like a flying saucer. It was interested in a murderer."

Mrs. Norman had Peter's social service files on the table in front of her. She leafed through them, obviously not paying much attention to Whelye. The chaplain, Hardwicke, had taken Thurlow's own psychometry file on Peter, but wasn't studying it. He seemed to be interested in the play of a sprinkler visible out the window at his right.

"Could you tell us your general attitude today, Peter?" Whelye asked. "How do you feel?"

"Oh, I'm all right."

"Are you still working in the sewing room? Seems to me you'd be more interested in that kind of work outside."

"Yes, I'm working there. I've been working there ever since I came."

"How long have you been here?"

"Pert' near two years now."

"How do you like it here?"

"Oh, it's all right. But I been wondering when you're going to let me out . . . so I can get back home an' help support my mother."

"Well, that's one thing we have you in here for," Whelye said, "so we can think it over."

"Well, that's what they been telling me for six months, now," Peter said. "Why do I have to stay here? The chaplain" (Peter shot a covert glance at Hardwicke) "told me you were going to write my mother to see if she wanted me home. An' if she did want me home, he'd take me down there."

"We haven't heard from your mother yet."

"Well, I got a letter from my mother an' she says she wants me home. The chaplain said if you'd let me go he'd take me home. So I don't see any reason why I can't go."

"It's not a simple decision, Peter. It's not just the chaplain's decision."

Hardwicke opened the psychometry file, made a pretense of studying it. Thurlow sighed, shook his head.

What was that thing I saw? Thurlow wondered. *Was it real there beside Murphey's window? Was it illusion?* The question had been plaguing him for two days.

"Well, he said he'd take me," Peter said.

Whelye stared at Hardwicke, disapproval on his face. "Did you say you'd take him down to Mariposa?"

"*If* he were discharged," Hardwicke said. "I said I'd be glad to give him the trip down there."

Whelye faced Peter, said: "Well, we have to do some more looking into this matter, generally to find out if your mother wants you and if the chaplain's schedule will allow him to take you down there. If all these things work out, we'll let you go."

Peter was sitting very still now, no emotion on his face, his gaze intent upon his hands. "Thank you."

"That's all, Peter," Whelye said. "You can go now."

Mrs. Norman signaled an attendant waiting at the screened window to the Common Room. The attendant opened the door. Peter got up and hurried out.

Thurlow sat for a moment, the realization growing in him that Peter had taken away what amounted to a promise to be released, but that because of the way he had conducted the conference, Dr. Whelye wasn't aware of this. Whelye would be thinking that all the "ifs" involved made this a hypothetical case.

"Well, Dr. Whelye," Thurlow said, "you've made a definite commitment to this patient to discharge him—promptly."

"Oh, no—I didn't promise I'd discharge him."

"Well, the patient certainly understood he'd be home in short order—and the only qualifications are Chaplain Hardwicke's schedule and confirmation of the mother's letter."

"Call the patient back and we'll settle this with him right now," Whelye said. He looked angry.

Mrs. Norman sighed, went to the Common Room

door, signaled an attendant. Peter was brought back and returned to his chair. The boy kept his eyes down, shoulders bent, unmoving.

"You understand, don't you, Peter," Whelye asked, "that we haven't made any definite promise to discharge you? We're going to look into your home situation and see if everything is all right and if you can get a job. We'd also like to look into the possibility of you returning to school for a year or so. Perhaps you could get a better job. You understand, don't you, that we aren't making any definite commitment?"

"Yeah, I understand." Peter looked at Chaplain Hardwicke who refused to meet the boy's gaze.

"What's this about school?" Thurlow asked.

"The boy hasn't finished high school," Whelye said. He faced Peter. "Wouldn't you like to go back and finish high school?"

"Yeah."

"Do you like to go to school?" Whelye asked.

"Yeah."

"Wouldn't you like to finish your education and get a job where you could pay your own way and save money and get married?"

"Yeah."

Whelye glanced triumphantly at Thurlow. "Anybody got any questions?"

Thurlow had slowly been building up in his mind the analogy of a stud poker game. Peter was in the position of a player who didn't believe anything happening here, nor did he *dis*believe anything. He was waiting to see the rest of the cards.

"Isn't it true, Peter," Thurlow asked, "that you'd rather be hungry than on a full stomach?"

"Yeah." The boy had turned his attention to Whelye now.

"Isn't it true, Peter," Thurlow asked, "that you'd rather eat a dry crust of bread than have a nice juicy piece of meat on your dinner plate?"

"Yeah."

"That's all," Thurlow said.

At Mrs. Norman's signal, the attendant took Peter once more from the room.

"I think when we get to the next patient," Thurlow said, "we should swear him in like they do in court."

Whelye remained silent for a moment. He shuffled his papers, then: "I don't see what you're driving at."

"You reminded me of a district attorney of my acquaintance," Thurlow said.

"Oh?" Whelye's eyes glazed with anger.

"By the way," Thurlow said, "do you believe in flying saucers?"

The heads of both Mrs. Norman and Chaplain Hardwicke snapped up. They stared at Thurlow. Whelye, however, drew back, his eyes veiled, watchful.

"What is the meaning of that question?" Whelye demanded.

"I'd like to know your position," Thurlow said.

"On flying saucers?" There was a cautious disbelief in Whelye's tone.

"Yes."

"They're delusional material," Whelye said. "Utter nonsense. Oh, there could be a few cases of mistaken identity, weather balloons and that sort of thing, but the people who insist they've seen spaceships, these people are in need of our services."

"A sound opinion," Thurlow said. "I'm glad to hear it."

Whelye nodded. "I don't care what you think of my methods," he said, "but you're not going to find my opinions based on delusional material—of *any* type. Is that clear?"

"Quite clear," Thurlow said. He saw that Whelye was convinced the question had carried a subtle intent to discredit.

Whelye got to his feet, glanced at his watch. "I fail to see the point in all this, but doubtless you had some idea in mind." He left the room.

Mrs. Norman took a deep breath, bent a look of sympathy on Thurlow. "You like to play with fire, evidently," she said.

Thurlow stood up, smiled.

Hardwicke, catching Thurlow's eyes, said: "The defense rests."

As the scene passed through his mind, Thurlow

shook his head. Again, he glanced at his wristwatch, smiled at himself as the unconscious gesture displayed the stopped hands. The air coming in the car window smelled of wet leaves.

Why did Ruth ask me to meet her here? She's another man's wife now. Where is she—so damned late! Could something have happened to her?

He looked at his pipe.

Damn' pipe's gone out. Always going out. I smoke matches, not tobacco. Hate to burn myself with this woman again. Poor Ruth—tragedy, tragedy. She was very close to her mother.

He tried to remember the murdered woman. Adele Murphey was photographs and descriptions in stories now, a reflection from the words of witnesses and police. The Adele Murphey he'd known refused to come out from behind the brutal new images. Her features were beginning to grow dim in the leaf whirl of things that fade. His mind held only the police pictures now—color photos in the file at the sheriff's office—the red hair (so much like the daughter's) fanned out on an oil-stained driveway.

Her bloodless skin in the photo—he remembered that.

And he remembered the words of the witness, Sarah French, the doctor's wife from next door, words on a deposition. Through Mrs. French's words, he could almost visualize that violent scene. Sarah French had heard shouting, a scream. She'd looked out of her second floor bedroom window onto moon-flooded night just in time to see the murder.

"Adele . . . Mrs. Murphey came running out of her back door. She was wearing a green nightgown . . . very thin. She was barefooted. I remember thinking how odd: she's barefooted. Then Joe was right behind her. He had that damned Malay kriss. It looked horrible, horrible. I could see his face . . . the moonlight. He looked like he always looks when he's angry. He has such a terrible temper!"

Sarah's words—Sarah's words. . . . Thurlow could almost see that zigzag blade glinting in Joe Murphey's hand, a vicious, shivering, wavering thing in the mottled shadows. It had taken Joe no more than ten steps to catch his wife. Sarah had counted the blows.

"I just stood there counting each time he struck her. I don't know why. I just counted. Seven times. Seven times."

Adele had sprawled onto the concrete, her hair spreading in that uneven splash which the cameras later recorded. Her knees had drawn up into a fetal curve, then straightened.

And all that time, the doctor's wife had been standing there at the upstairs window, left hand to mouth, her flesh a rigid, mortal concrete.

"I couldn't move. I couldn't even speak. All I could do was just watch him."

Joe Murphey's oddly thin-wristed right hand had come up, hurled the kriss in a short arc onto the lawn. Unhurriedly, he had walked around his wife's body, avoided the spreading patch of red that trailed down the concrete. Presently, he'd merged with the shadows of trees where the driveway entered the street. Sarah had heard a car motor start. Its lights had flashed on. The car had roared away in a gritty scattering of gravel.

Then, and only then, Sarah had found she could move. She'd called an ambulance.

"Andy?"

The voice brought Thurlow back from a far distance. *Ruth's voice?* he wondered. He turned.

She stood at his left just behind the car, a slender woman in a black silk suit that smoothed her full curves. Her red hair, usually worn close around her oval face, was tied in a severe coil at the back of her neck. The hair bound so tightly—Thurlow tried to put out of his mind all memory of the mother's hair spread on the driveway.

Ruth's green eyes stared at him with a look of hurt expectancy. She had the appearance of a tired elf.

Thurlow opened his door, slipped out to the wet grass beside the road.

"I didn't hear your car," he said.

"I've been staying with Sarah, living with her. I walked up from the house. That's why I'm so late."

He could hear the tears in her voice and wondered at the inanity of their conversation.

"Ruth . . . damn it all! I don't know what to say." Without thinking about it, he crossed to her, took her in his arms. He could feel her muscles resisting him. "I don't know what to say."

She pulled out of his embrace. "Then . . . don't say anything. It's all been said anyway." She looked up at his eyes. "Aren't you still wearing your special glasses?"

"To hell with my glasses. Why wouldn't you speak to me on the phone? Was that Sarah's number they gave me at the hospital?" Her words were coming back to him, ". . . living with her." What did it mean?

"Father said. . . ." She bit her lower lip, shook her head. "Andy, oh, Andy, he's insane and they're going to execute him. . . ." She looked up at Thurlow, her lashes wet with tears. "Andy, I don't know how to feel about him. I don't know. . . ."

Again, he took her in his arms. She came willingly this time. How familiar and right it felt for her to be there. She began to sob gently against his shoulder. Her crying felt like the spent aftermath of sorrow.

"Oh, I wish you could take me away from here," she whispered.

What was she saying? he asked himself. She was no longer Ruth Murphey. She was Mrs. Neville Hudson. He wanted to push her away, start throwing questions at her. But that wouldn't be professional, not the right *psychological* thing to do. He decided it wasn't what he wanted to do after all. Still, she was another man's wife. Damn! Damn! Damn! What had happened? The flight. He remembered their fight—the night he'd told her about the followship grant. She hadn't wanted him to take it, to be separated for a year. Denver had sounded so far away in her words. *"It's only a year."* He could hear his own voice saying it. *"You think more of your damn' career than you do of me!"* The temper matched her hair.

He'd left on that sour note. His letters had gone into a void—unanswered. She'd been "not home" to his telephone calls. And he'd learned he could be angry, too—and hurt. But what had really happened?

Again, she said: "I don't know how to feel about him."

"What can I do to help?" It was all he could say, but the words felt inadequate.

She pushed away from him. "Anthony Bondelli, the attorney—we've hired him. He wants to talk to you. I . . . I told him about your report on . . . father—the time he turned in the false fire alarm." Her face crumpled. "Oh, Andy—why did you go away? I needed you. We needed you."

"Ruth . . . , your father wouldn't take any help from me."

"I know. He hated you . . . because of . . . what you said. But he still needed you."

"Nobody listened to me, Ruth. He was too important a man for. . . ."

"Bondelli thinks you can help with the insanity plea. He asked me to see you, to. . . ." She shrugged, pulled a handkerchief from her pocket, wiped her cheeks.

So that's it, Thurlow thought. *She's making up to me to get my help, buying my help!*

He turned away to hide his sudden anger and the pain. For a moment, his eyes didn't focus, then he grew aware (quite slowly, it seemed) of a subtle brownian movement at the edge of the grove. It was like a swarm of gnats, but unlike them too. His glasses. Where were his glasses? In the car! The *gnats* dissolved away upward. Their retreat coincided with the lifting of an odd pressure from his senses, as though a sound or something like a sound had been wearing on his nerves, but now was gone.

"You will help?" Ruth asked.

Was that the same sort of thing I saw at Murphey's window? Thurlow asked himself. *What is it?*

Ruth took a step nearer, looked up at his profile. "Bondelli thought—because of us—you might . . . hesitate."

The damned pleading in her voice! His mind replayed her question. He said: "Yes, I'll help any way I can."

"That man . . . in the jail is just a shell," she said. Her voice was low, flat, almost without expression. He looked down at her, seeing how her features drew inward as she spoke. "He's not my father. He just looks like my father. My father's dead. He's been dead . . . for a long time. We didn't realize it . . . that's all."

God! How pitiful she looked!

"I'll do everything I can," he said, "but. . . ."

"I know there isn't much hope," she said. "I know how they feel—the people. It was my mother this man killed."

"People sense he's insane," Thurlow said, his voice unconsciously taking a pedantic tone. "They know it from the way he talks—from what he did. Insanity is, unfortunately, a communicable disease. He's aroused a counter-insanity. He's an irritant the community wants removed. He raises questions about themselves that people can't answer."

"We shouldn't be talking about him," she said. "Not here." She looked around the grove. "But I have to talk about him—or go crazy."

"That's quite natural," he said, his voice carefully soothing. "The disturbance *he* created, the community disturbance is. . . . Damn it! Words are so stupid sometimes!"

"I know," she said. "I can take the clinical approach, too. If my . . . if that man in the jail should be judged insane and sent to a mental hospital, people'd have to ask themselves very disturbing questions."

"Can a person appear sane when he's really insane?" Thurlow said. "Can a man be insane when he thinks he's sane? Could *I* be insane enough to do the things this man did?"

"I'm through crying now," she said. She glanced up at Thurlow, looked away. "The daughter's had her fill of . . . sorrow. I. . . ." She took a deep breath. "I can . . . hate . . . for the way my mother died. But I'm still a psychiatric nurse and I know all the professional cant. None of it helps the daughter much. It's odd—as though I were more than one person."

Again, she looked up at Thurlow, her expression open, without any defenses. "And I can run to the man I love and ask him to take me away from here because I'm afraid . . . deathly afraid."

The man I love! Her words seared his mind. He shook his head. "But . . . what about. . . ."

"Nev?" How bitter she made the name sound. "I haven't lived with Nev for three months now. I've been staying with Sarah French. Nev . . . Nev was a hideous mistake. That *grasping* little man!"

Thurlow found his throat was tight with suppressed emotion. He coughed, looked up at the darkening sky, said: "It'll be dark in a few minutes." How stupidly inane the words sounded!

She put a hand on his arm. "Andy, oh Andy, what've I done to us?"

She came into his arms very gently. He stroked her hair. "We're still here," he said. "We're still us."

Ruth looked up at him. "The trouble with that man in the jail is he has a *sane* type of delusion." Tears were running down her cheeks, but her voice remained steady. "He thinks my mother was unfaithful to him. Lots of men worry about that. I imagine . . . even . . . Nev could worry about that."

A sudden gust of wind shook raindrops off the leaves, spattering them.

Ruth freed herself from his arms. "Let's walk out to the point."

"In the dark?"

"We know the way. Besides, the riding club has lights there now. You see them every night across the valley from the hospital. They're automatic."

"It's liable to rain."

"Then it won't matter if I cry. My cheeks'll already be wet."

"Ruth . . . honey . . . I. . . ."

"Just take me for a walk the way . . . we used to."

Still he hesitated. There was something frightening about the grove . . . pressure, an *almost* sound. He stepped to the car, reached in and found his glasses. He slipped them on, looked around—nothing. No *gnats,* not a sign of anything odd—except the pressure.

"You won't need your glasses," Ruth said. She took his arm.

Thurlow found he couldn't speak past a sudden ache

in his throat. He tried to analyze his fear. It wasn't a personal thing. He decided he was afraid *for* Ruth.

"Come on," she said.

He allowed her to lead him across the grass toward the bridle path. Darkness came like a sharp demarcation as they emerged from the eucalyptus grove onto the first rise up through pines and buckeyes that hemmed the riding club's trail. Widely spaced night-riding lights attached to the trees came on with a wet glimmering through drenched leaves. In spite of the afternoon's rain, the duff-packed trail felt firm underfoot.

"We'll have the trail to ourselves tonight," Ruth said. "No one'll be out because of the rain." She squeezed his arm.

But we don't have it to ourselves, Thurlow thought. He could feel a presence with them—a hovering something . . . watchful, dangerous. He looked down at Ruth. The top of her head came just above his shoulder. The red hair glinted wetly in the dim overhead light. There was a feeling of damp silence around them—and that odd sense of pressure. The packed duff of the trail absorbed their footfalls with barely a sound.

This is a crazy feeling, he thought. *If a patient described this to me, I'd begin probing immediately for the source of the delusional material.*

"I used to walk up here when I was a child," Ruth said. "That was before they put in the lights for the night parties. I hated it when they put in the lights."

"You walked here in the dark?" he asked.

"Yes. I never told you that, did I?"

"No."

"The air feels clear after the rain." She took a deep breath.

"Didn't your parents object? How old were you?"

"About eleven, I guess. My parents didn't know. They were always so busy with parties and things."

The bridle path diverged at a small glade with a dark path leading off to the left through an opening in a rock retaining wall. They went through the gap, down a short flight of steps and onto the tarred top of an elevated water storage tank. Below them the city's lights spread wet velvet jewels across the night. The lights cast an orange glow against low hanging clouds.

Now, Thurlow could feel the odd pressure intensely. He looked up and around—nothing. He glanced down at the pale grayness of Ruth's face.

"When we got here you used to say: 'May I kiss you?' " she said. "And I used to say: 'I was hoping you'd ask.' "

Ruth turned, pressed against him, lifted her face. His fears, the vague pressure, all were forgotten as he bent to kiss her. It seemed for a moment that time had moved backward, that Denver, Nev—none of these things had happened. But the warmth of her kiss, the demanding way her body pressed against him—these filled him with a mounting astonishment. He pulled away.

"Ruth, I . . ."

She put a finger against his lips. "Don't say it." Then: "Andy, didn't you ever want to go to a motel with me?"

"Hell! Lots of times, but. . . ."

"You've never made a real pass at me."

He felt that she was laughing at him and this brought anger into his voice. "I was in love with you!"

"I know," she whispered.

"I didn't want just a roll in the hay. I wanted . . . well, dammit, I wanted to *mate* with you, have children, the whole schmoo."

"What a fool I was," she whispered.

"Honey, what're you going to do? Are you going to get . . . a. . . ." He hesitated.

"A divorce?" she asked. "Of course—afterward."

"After the . . . trial."

"Yes."

"That's the trouble with a small town," he said. "Everyone knows everyone else's business even when it's none of their business."

"For a psychologist, that's a very involved sentence," she said. She snuggled against him and they stood there silently while Thurlow remembered the vague pressure and probed for it in his mind as though it were a sore tooth. Yes, it was still there. When he relaxed his guard, a deep disquiet filled him.

"I keep thinking about my mother," Ruth said.

"Oh?"

"She loved my father, too."

Coldness settled in his stomach. He started to speak, remained silent as his eyes detected movement against the orange glow of clouds directly in front of him. An object settled out of the clouds and came to a hovering stop about a hundred yards away and slightly above their water-tank vantage point. Thurlow could define the thing's shape against the background glow—four shimmering tubular legs beneath a fluorescing green dome. A rainbow circle of light whirled around the base of each leg.

"Andy! You're hurting me!"

He realized he had locked his arms around her in a spasm of shock. Slowly, he released his grip.

"Turn around," he whispered. "Tell me what you see out there against the clouds."

She gave him a puzzled frown, turned to peer out toward the city. "Where?"

"Slightly above us—straight ahead against the clouds."

"I don't see anything."

The object began drifting nearer. Thurlow could distinguish figures behind the green dome. They moved in a dim, phosphorescent light. The rainbow glow beneath the thing's tubular legs began to fade.

"What're you looking at?" Ruth asked. "What is it?"

He felt her trembling beneath his hand on her shoulder. "Right there," he said, pointing. "Look, right there."

She bent to stare along his arm. "I don't see a thing—just clouds."

He wrenched off his glasses. "Here. Look through these." Even without the glasses, Thurlow could see the thing's outline. It coasted along the edge of the hill—nearer . . . nearer.

Ruth put on the glasses, looked where he pointed. "I . . . a dark blur of some kind," she said. "It looks like

... smoke or a cloud ... or ... insects. Is it a swarm of insects?"

Thurlow's mouth felt dry. There was a painful constricting sensation in his throat. He reclaimed his glasses, looked at the drifting object. The figures inside were quite distinct now. He counted five of them, the great staring eyes all focused on him.

"Andy! What is it you see?"

"You're going to think I'm nuts."

"What is it?"

He took a deep breath, described the object.

"Five men in it?"

"Perhaps they're men, but they're very small. They look no more than three feet tall."

"Andy, you're frightening me. Why are you frightening me?"

"I'm frightening myself."

She pressed back into his arms. "Are you sure you see this ... this ... I can't see a thing."

"I see them as plainly as I see you. If it's illusion, it's a most complete illusion."

The rainbow glow beneath the tubular legs had become a dull blue. The object settled lower, lower, came to a hovering stop about fifteen yards away and level with them.

"Maybe it's a new kind of helicopter," Ruth said. "Or ... Andy, I still can't see it."

"Describe what you see ..." He pointed ". . . right there."

"A little mistiness. It looks like it's going to rain again."

"They're working with a square machine of some kind," he said. "It has what look like short antennae. The antennae glow. They're pointing it at us."

"Andy, I'm scared." She was shivering in his arms.

"I ... think we'd better get out of here," he said. He willed himself to leave, found he couldn't move.

"I ... can't ... move," Ruth whispered.

He could hear her teeth chattering, but his own body felt frozen in dull cement.

"Andy, I can't move!" There was hysteria in her voice. "Is it still there?"

"They're pointing some device at us," he husked. His voice felt as though it came from far away, from another person. "They're doing this to us. Are you *sure* you can't see anything?"

"Nothing! A misty little cloud, nothing else."

Thurlow felt suddenly that she was just being obstinate. Anyone could see the thing right there in front of them! Intense anger at her surged through him. Why wouldn't she admit she saw it? Right there! He hated her for being so obstinate. The irrational abruptness of the emotion asserted itself in his awareness. He began to question his own reaction.

How could I feel hate for Ruth? I love her.

As though this thought freed him, Thurlow found he could move his legs. He began backing away, dragging Ruth with him. She was a heavy, unmoving weight. Her feet scraped against the gravel in the tank's surface.

His movement set off a flurry of activity among the creatures beneath the green dome. They buzzed and fussed over their square machine. A painful constriction seized Thurlow's chest. Each breath took a laboring concentration. Still, he continued backing away dragging Ruth with him. She sagged in his arms now. His foot encountered a step and he almost fell. Slowly, he began inching backward up the steps. Ruth was a dead weight.

"Andy," she gasped. "Can't . . . breathe."

"Hold . . . on," he rasped.

They were at the top of the steps now, then back through the gap in the stone wall. Movement became somewhat easier, although he could still see the domed object hovering beyond the water storage tank. The glowing antennae remained pointed at him.

Ruth began to move her legs. She turned, and they hobbled together onto the bridle path. Each step grew easier. Thurlow could hear her taking deep, sighing breaths. Abruptly, as though a weight had been lifted from them, they regained full use of their muscles.

They turned.

"It's gone," Thurlow said.

She reacted with an anger that astonished him.

"What were you trying to pull back there, Andy Thurlow? Frightening me half out of my wits!"

"I saw what I told you I saw," he said. "You may not've seen it, but you certainly felt it."

"Hysterical paralysis," she said.

"It gripped us both at the same instant and left us both at the same instant," he said.

"Why not?"

"Ruth, I saw exactly what I described."

"Flying saucers!" she sneered.

"No . . . well, maybe. But it was there!" He was angry now, defensive. A rational part of him saw how insane the past few minutes had been. Could it have been illusion? No! He shook his head. "Honey, I saw. . . ."

"Don't you *honey* me!"

He grabbed her shoulders, shook her. "Ruth! Two minutes ago you were saying you love me. Can you turn it off just like that?"

"I. . . ."

"Does somebody want you to hate me?"

"What?" She stared up at him, her face dim in the tree lights.

"Back there . . ." He nodded toward the tank. "I felt myself angry with you . . . hating you. I told myself I couldn't hate you. I love you. That's when I found I could move. But when I felt the . . . hate, the instant I felt it, that was exactly when they pointed their machine at us."

"What machine?"

"Some kind of box with glowing rods or antennae sticking out of it."

"Are you trying to tell me that those nutty . . . *whatever* could make you feel hate . . . or. . . ."

"That's how it felt."

"That's the craziest thing I ever heard!" She backed away from him.

"I know it's crazy, but that's how it felt." He reached for her arm. "Let's get back to the car."

Ruth pulled away. "I'm not going a step with you until you explain what happened out there."

"I can't explain it."

"How could you see it when I couldn't?"

"Maybe the accident . . . my eyes, the polarizing glasses."

"Are you sure that accident at the radlab didn't injure more than your eyes?"

He suppressed a surge of anger. It was so easy to feel angry. With some difficulty, he held his voice level. "They had me on the artificial kidney for a week and with every test known to God and man. The burst altered the ion exchange system in the cones of my retinas. That's all. And it isn't permanent. But I think whatever happened to my eyes, that's why I can see these things. I'm not supposed to see them, but I can."

Again, he reached for her, captured her arm. Half dragging her, he set off down the path. She fell into step beside him.

"But what could they be?" she asked.

"I don't know, but they're real. Trust me, Ruth. Trust that much. They're real." He knew he was begging and hated himself for it, but Ruth moved closer, tucked her arm under his.

"All right, darling, I trust you. You saw what you saw. What're you going to do about it?"

They came off the trail and into the eucalyptus grove. The car was a darker shape among shadows. Thurlow drew her to a stop beside it.

"How hard is it to believe me?" he asked.

She was silent for a moment, then: "It's . . . difficult."

"Okay," he said. "Kiss me."

"What?"

"Kiss me. Let's see if you really hate me."

"Andy, you're being. . . ."

"Are you afraid to kiss me?"

"Of course not!"

"Okay then." He pulled her to him. Their lips met. For an instant, he sensed resistance, then she melted into his embrace, her arms creeping behind his neck.

Presently, he drew away.

"If that's hate, I want lots of it," he said.

"Me, too."

Again, she pressed herself against him.

Thurlow felt his blood pounding. He pulled away with an abrupt, defensive motion.

"Sometimes I wish you weren't so damned Victorian," she said. "But maybe I wouldn't love you then."

He brushed a strand of the red hair away from her cheek. How faintly glowing her face looked in the light from the bridle trail lamps behind him. "I think I'd better take you home . . . to Sarah."

"I don't want you to take me home."

"I don't want you to go home."

"But I'd better?"

"You'd better."

She put her hands against his chest, pushed away.

They got into the car, moving with a sudden swift embarrassment. Thurlow started the engine, concentrated on backing to the turn-around. The headlights picked out lines of crusty brown bark on the trees. Abruptly, the headlights went dark. The engine died with a gasping cough. A breathless, oppressive sensation seized him.

"Andy!" Ruth said. "What's happening?"

Thurlow forced himself to turn to the left, wondering how he knew where to look. There were four rainbow glows close to the ground, the tubular legs and the green dome just outside the grove. The thing hovered there, silent, menacing.

"They're back," he whispered. "Right there." He pointed.

"Andy . . . Andy, I'm frightened." She huddled against him.

"No matter what happens, you don't hate me," he said. "You love me. Remember that. You love me. Keep it in your mind."

"I love you." Her voice was faint.

A directionless sense of anger began to fill Thurlow. It had no object at first. Just anger. Then he could actually feel it trying to point at Ruth.

"I . . . want to . . . hate you," she whispered.

"You love me," he said. "Don't forget that."

"I love you. Oh, Andy, I love you. I don't want to hate you . . . I love you."

Thurlow lifted a fist, shook it at the green dome.

"Hate them," he rasped. "Hate bastards who'd try to manipulate us that way."

He could feel her shaking and trembling against his shoulder. "I . . . hate . . . them," she said.

"Now, do you believe me?"

"Yes! Yes, I believe you!"

"Could the car have hysterical paralysis?"

"No. Oh, Andy, I couldn't just turn on hate against you. I couldn't." His arm ached where she clutched it. "What are they? My God! What is it?"

"I don't think they're human," Thurlow said.

"What're we going to do?"

"Anything we can."

The rainbow circles beneath the dome shifted into the blue, then violet and into the red. The thing began to lift away from the grove. It receded into the darkness. With it went the sense of oppression.

"It's gone, isn't it?" Ruth whispered.

"It's gone."

"Your lights are on," she said.

He looked down at the dash lights, out at the twin cones of the headlights stabbing into the grove.

He recalled the shape of the thing then—like a giant spider ready to pounce on them. He shuddered. What were the creatures in that ominous machine?

Like a giant spider.

His mind dredged up a memory out of childhood: *Oberon's palace has walls of spider's legs.*

Were they faerie, the huldu-folk?

Where did the myths originate? he wondered. He could feel his mind questing down old paths and he remembered a verse from those days of innocence—

> "See ye not yon bonny road
>   That winds about yon fernie brae?
>   That is the road to fair Elfland
>   Where thou and I this night maun gae."

"Hadn't we better go?" Ruth asked.

He started the engine, his hands moving automatically through the kinesthetic pattern.

"It stopped the motor and turned off the lights," Ruth said. "Why would they do that?"

They! he thought. *No doubts now.*

He headed the car out of the grove down the hill toward Moreno Drive.

"What're we going to do?" Ruth asked.

"Can we do anything?"

"If we talk about it, people'll say we're crazy. Besides . . . the two of us . . . up here. . . ."

We're neatly boxed, he thought. And he imagined what Whelye would say to a recountal of this night's experiences. *"You were with another man's wife, you say? Could guilt feelings have brought on this shared delusion?"* And if this met with protests and further suggestions—*"Faerie folk? My dear Thurlow, do you feel well?"*

Ruth leaned against him. "Andy, if they could make us hate, could they make us love?"

He swerved the car over to the shoulder of the road, turned off the motor, set the handbrake, extinguished the lights. "They're not here right now."

"How do we know?"

He stared around at the night—blackness, not even starlight under those clouds . . . no glow of weird object—but beyond the trees bordering the road . . . what?

Could they make us love?

Damn her for asking such a question!

No! I mustn't damn her. I must love her . . . I . . . must.

"Andy? What're you doing?"

"Thinking."

"Andy, even with us—I still find this whole thing so unreal. Couldn't there be some other explanation? I mean, your motor stopping. . . . Motors do stop; lights go out. Don't they?"

"What do you want from me?" he asked. "Do you want me to say yes, I'm nuts, I'm deluded. I'm. . . ."

She put a hand over his mouth. "What I want is for you to make love to me and never stop."

He started to put an arm around her, but she pushed

him away. "No. When that happens, I want to know it's us making love, not someone forcing us."

Damn her practicality! he thought. Then: *No! I love her . . . but is it me loving her? Is it my own doing?*

"Andy? There is something you can do for me."

"What?"

"The house on Manchester Avenue . . . where Nev and I were living—there're some things I want from there, but I've been afraid to go over there alone. Would you take me?"

"Now?"

"It's early yet. Nev may still be down at the plant. My . . . father made him assistant manager, you know. Hasn't anyone told you that's why he married me? To get the business."

Thurlow put a hand on her arm. "You want him to know . . . about us?"

"What's there to know?"

He returned his hand to the steering wheel. "Okay, darling. As you say."

Again, he started the motor, pulled the car onto the road. They drove in silence. The tires hissed against wet pavement. Other cars passed, their lights glaring. Thurlow adjusted the polarizing lenses. It was a delicate thing—to give him enough visibility but prevent the pain of sudden light.

Presently, Ruth said: "I don't want any trouble, a fight. You wait for me in the car. If I need help, I'll call."

"You're sure you don't want me to go in with you?"

"He won't try anything if he knows you're there."

He shrugged. She was probably right. Certainly, she must know Nev Hudson's character by now. But Thurlow still felt a nagging sensation of suspended judgment. He suspected the events of the past few days, even the menacing encounter of this night, made some odd kind of sense.

"Why did I marry him?" Ruth asked. "I keep asking myself. God knows. I don't. It just seemed to come to the point where. . . ." She shrugged. "After tonight, I wonder if any of us knows why we do what we do."

She looked up at Thurlow. "Why is this happening, darling?"

That's it, Thurlow thought. *There's the sixty-four dollar question. It's not Who are these creatures? It's . . . what do they want? Why are they interfering in our lives?*

8

FRAFFIN GLARED AT THE IMAGE PROJECTED ABOVE HIS
desk. It was Lutt, his Master-of-Craft, a broad-faced
Chem, steely skinned, harsh and abrupt in his decisions, lacking subtlety. He combined all the best qualities for one who supervised the mechanical end of this
work, but those very qualities interfered with his
present assignment. He obviously equated subtlety with
caution.

A moment of silence served to acquaint Lutt with
the Director's displeasure. Fraffin felt the contour
pressures of his chair, glanced at the silvery web of the
pantovive across the salon. Yes, Lutt was like that instrument. He had to be *activated* correctly.

Fraffin ran a finger along his jaw, said: "I didn't tell
you to spare the immune. You were directed to bring
the female here—at once!"

"If I have erred, I abase myself," Lutt said. "But I
acted on the basis of past directives concerning this immune. The way you gave his female to another, the
way you. . . ."

"He was an amusing diversion, no more," Fraffin
said. "Kelexel has asked to *examine* a native and he
has mentioned this female specifically by name. She is
to be brought here at once, unharmed. That proviso
doesn't apply to *any* other native who tries to interfere
or delay you in the execution of this order. Am I understood?"

"The Director is understood," Lutt said. There was
fear in his voice. Lutt knew the possible consequences
of Fraffin's displeasure: dismissal from a position of
unlimited delights and diversions, from a life that never
bored. He lived in a Chem paradise from which he

could easily be shunted to some tertiary post and with no recourse because they shared the same guilt, he and Fraffin, the same guilt with its certain terrible punishment if they were ever discovered.

"Without delay," Fraffin said.

"She will be here before this shift is half spent," Lutt said. "I go to obey."

Lutt's image faded, disappeared.

Fraffin leaned back. It was going fairly well ... in spite of this delay. Imagine that Lutt trying to separate the lovers by manipulating their emotions! The clod must know the danger of trying that on an immune. Well, the female would be here soon and Kelexel could examine her as he wished. Every tool and device to bend the native's will would be provided, of course—as a matter of courtesy. Let no one question the hopsitality of Fraffin the Director.

Fraffin chuckled.

Let the stupid investigator try the pleasures of this native. Let him impregnate the female. His flesh would know it when it was done. Accomplished breeding would accelerate his need for rejuvenation and where could he turn? Could he go back to the Primacy and say: "Rejuvenate me; I've produced an unlicensed child"? His flesh wouldn't permit that—no more than would the Primacy with its hidebound absolutes.

Oh, no. Kelexel would know the storyship had its own Rejuvenators, its own surgeon. He'd come begging, his mind telling him: *"I can have as many children as I wish and damn the Primacy!"* Once he'd been rejuvenated, the storyship would own him.

Again, Fraffin chuckled.

They might even get back to the lovely little war in time to make a complete production out of it.

9

RUTH WAS SURPRISED TO FIND HERSELF ENJOYING THE anger that condensed the room around her. The frustrated emotion that had built up in her out there in the night with Andy had an outlet at last. She watched the nervous twisting of Nev's pink hands with their baby-skin creases at the knuckles. She knew how his hands betrayed his feelings no matter what the masked rest of him revealed. Eight months of living with the man had given her considerable knowledge. Words came out of her full lips now like slivers of bamboo to be inserted beneath Nev's manicured soul.

"Scream about your husband's rights all you want," she said. "The business is mine now and I don't want you anywhere near it. Ohhh, I know why you married me. You didn't fool me for long, Nev. Not for long."

"Ruth, you. . . ."

"No more! Andy's out there waiting for me. I'm going to take the few things I want here and I'm leaving."

Nev's wide high forehead creased. The shoe-button eyes stared at her with their matched nothingness. *On one of her rampages again, that's all. And enjoying it, damn her! I can tell by the way she shakes her head like a horse . . . whores . . . horse . . . whores—a horsey, high-class whore.*

Ruth broke her gaze away from him. Nev frightened her when he stared that way. She studied the room, wondering if there were anything here she wanted now. Nothing. It was a Nev Hudson room with overlapping muted reds and browns, Oriental bric-a-brac, a grand piano in one corner, a closed violin case that opened to reveal three bottles of liquor and a set of glasses. Nev liked that. *"Let's get drunk and make beautiful music, honey."* Windows beyond the piano stood uncurtained to the night and garden lights, lawn, barbecue pit, wrought iron furniture standing whitely dripping after the rain.

"California is a community-property state," Nev said.

"You'd better look into the law again," she said. "The business is my inheritance."

"Inheritance?" he asked. "But your father's not dead yet."

She stood staring at the night, refusing to let him goad her.

Damn her! he thought. *I should've done better in a woman but not with a business thrown into the bargain. She's thinking about that bastard Andy Thurlow. She wants him but she needs my brains running the business. That ugly stick of a boy-man in her bed! She won't have him; I'll see to it.*

"If you go away with this *Dr.* Thurlow, I'll ruin him professionally and I'll ruin you," he said.

She turned her head sideways, presenting a Greek profile, the severe line of her red hair tied at the back. A barely perceptible smile touched her lips, was gone. "Jealous, Nev?"

"I've warned you."

"You married me for the business," she said. "What do you care how I spend my time?" And she turned toward him. *Squirm, you little pig of a man! What was I thinking of? What was I ever thinking of to take you instead of Andy. Did something twist my emotions, make me do it?* She felt suddenly weak with the hungry hating. *Is any choice ever right right right? Andy choosing that Fellowship instead of me, his eyes full of innocence oh hateful! Where did I spend my innocence? Unthinking about animal bodies and power. Did I choose power in Nev? But he let me take it away from him his own power and now I can hate him with it.*

"The daughter of a murderer!" he snapped.

She glared at him. *Is this what I chose? Why why why? Lonely, that's why. All alone when Andy left me for that damned Fellowship and there was Nev Nev Nev insistent kind kind like a fox. Drunk I was drunk and feeling hateful. Nev used my hate that's the only power he had—hate my hate my hate I mustn't hate then and he's powerless I won't even hate him putting his hand on my knee oh so kind so kind and a little higher and there we were in bed married and Andy away in Denver and I was still alone.*

"I'm going," she said. "Andy's going to drive me over to Sarah's. If you try to stop me, I'll call him in and I'm quite sure he can handle you."

Nev's narrow, purse-string mouth tightened. His shoe-button eyes betrayed a brief flaring and then the mask was back in place. *I'll ruin them both! The bitch prattling about Andy well I showed dear old honest Andy the boy with the built in system of honor and what would she say if she learned I was the one put on the pressure to get him that Fellowship?*

"You know what the town'll think," he said. "Like father like daughter. They'll take my side. You know that."

She stamped her foot. "You pig!"

Certainly, Ruth, my dear. Get angry and stamp around like a wonderful animal my god would I like to take you to bed right now angry and hurting throwing yourself and twisting and jerking my god you're splendid when you're angry. I'm better for you than Andy and you should know it we're two of a kind we take what we want and damn the honor no honor no honor on her on her on her what an animal when she's angry but that's what life's for to take to take and take and take until we're filled up on it and she raves about Andy going back to him but Andy doesn't take from me no siree I'll get rid of him just as easily as I did before and Ruthy'll come crawling back to her ever loving Nev who knows her right down to her adorable most angry adorable if I only had the guts to yank you into the bedroom right now . . . well, I'd get rid of Andy just like I did before.

"We'll strike a bargain," he said. "Go along with your lover, but don't interfere with how I run the business. You said it yourself: what do I care how you spend your time?"

Go ahead, compromise yourselves, he thought. *I'll own you.*

She whirled away, strode down the hall, jerked open the bedroom door, snapped on the light.

Nev was right behind her. He stood in the doorway watching as she yanked clothes from drawers and the closet, threw them on the bed.

"Well, what about it?" he asked.

She forced words out of her mouth, knowing they told more than she wanted to reveal. "All right! Keep the business . . . or whatever. We know what's precious to you." She turned to face him, near tears and fighting to hide it. "You're the most hateful creature I've ever met! You can't be human." She put a hand to her mouth. "I wonder if you are."

"What's that supposed to. . . ." He broke off, stared past her toward the French doors onto the patio. "Ruth. . . ." Her name came out in a strangled gasp.

She whirled.

The French doors stood open to reveal three squat figures clothed in green moving into the room. To Ruth, their heads seemed strangely large, the eyes faintly luminous and frightening. They carried short tubes of silvery metal. There was a disdainful sense of power in the purposeful way they fanned out, pointing those metal tubes casually at the bedroom's occupants.

Ruth found herself wondering with an odd feeling of surprise how they'd opened the French doors without her hearing it.

Behind her, Nev gasped, said: "See here! Who. . . ." His voice trailed off in a frightening hiss, an exhalation as though he were a punctured balloon. A liquid trilling sound poured from the mouth of the creature on Ruth's right.

This can't be happening, she thought. Then: *They're the creatures who frightened us in the grove! What do they want? What're they doing?*

She found suddenly that she couldn't move. Her head felt detached, mind clear, but there were no connections to her body. One of the creatures moved to stand directly in front of her—a queer little manling in green leotards, his torso partly concealed in a cloudy, bulging roundness that pulsed with a purple inner light. She remembered Andy's description of what he'd seen: *"Glowing eyes. . . ."*

Andy! She wanted to scream for him, but her voice wouldn't obey. How drifting and soft the world seemed!

Something jerked past her and she saw Nev there walking as though pulled by strings. Her eyes focused on a smudge of powder along his shoulder, a pulsing vein at his temple. He tipped forward suddenly in that strange marionette way, falling rigidly into one of the open French doors. There came the crash and tinkling of broken glass. The floor around him became bright with flowing red. He twitched, lay still.

The gnome creature in front of her spoke quite distinctly in English: "An accident, you see?"

She had no voice to answer, only a distant horror somewhere within the powdery billowing that was her self. Ruth closed her eyes, thinking: *Andy! Oh, Andy, help me!*

Again, she heard one of the creatures speak in that liquid trilling. She tried to open her eyes, couldn't. Waves of darkness began to wash over what remained of her awareness. As unconsciousness came, her mind focused clearly on a single oddly pertinent thought: *This can't be happening because no one would believe it. This is nightmare, that's all.*

10

THURLOW SAT IN THE DARK CAR SMOKING HIS PIPE, wondering what was taking Ruth so long in the house. *Should I go in after all?* he asked himself. *It isn't right that I stay out here while she's in there alone with him. But she said she could handle him.*

Did Adele think she could handle Joe?

That's a crazy thought!

It was raining again, a thin drizzle that misted the streetlight at the corner in front of him. He turned, glanced at the house—lights in the living room, but no sign of movement behind the drawn shades.

When she comes to the door, I'll go up and help her carry whatever . . . no! Dammit, I should go in now. But she must know if she can handle him.

Handle him!

What was it like, those two? Why did she marry him?

He shook his head, looked away from the house. The night appeared too dark beyond the streetlights and he eased off the setting on his polarizing lenses.

What was keeping her in there?

He thought suddenly of the hovering object he'd seen at the grove. *There must be some logical explanation*, he thought. *Perhaps if I called the Air Force . . . anonymously. . . . Somebody must have a simple, logical explanation.*

But what if they haven't?

My God! What if the saucer nuts turn out to've been right all along?

He tried to see his wristwatch, remembered it hadn't been wound. Damn she was taking a long time in there!

72

Like a train shunted onto an odd track, his mind veered to a memory of Ruth's father, the compelling directness of the man's eyes. *"Take care of Ruthy!"*

And that thing hovering at Joe's window—what had that been?

Thurlow took off his glasses, polished them with a handkerchief, slipped them back on his nose. He remembered Joe Murphey in April, right after the man had turned in the false fire alarm. What a shock it had been to find Ruth's father facing him in the dirty little examination room above the sheriff's office. And there'd been the even greater shock at evaluating the man's tests. The dry language of his report to the probation office couldn't begin to convey that shock.

"I found him to be a man lacking a good central core of balanced feelings. This, coupled to a dangerous compulsive element such as the false fire alarm, should be considered a warning of serious disturbance. Here is a man whose psychological makeup contains all the elements necessary for a terrible tragedy."

The language of the report—so careful in its wording, maintaining the strict esoterica of officialese . . . he'd known how little it might convey and had supplemented it with a verbal report.

"The man's dangerous. He's a definite paranoid type and could explode. He's capable of violence."

The disbelief had been frightening. "Surely this is nothing more than a prank. Joe Murphey! Hell, he's an important man here, Andy. Well . . . could you recommend analysis . . . psychoanalysis."

"He won't have anything to do with it . . . and I doubt it'd do him any good."

"Well, what do you expect us to do? Can't you recommend something?"

"Maybe we can get him into a church. I'll call Father Giles at the Episcopal church and see if. . . ."

"A church?"

Thurlow remembered his rueful shrug, the too pat words: "I'll probably be read out of the order for this, but religion often does what psychology can't."

Thurlow sighed. Father Giles, of course, had been unsuccessful.

Damn! What was keeping Ruth in that house? He reached for the car door, thought better of it. Give her a few more minutes. Everything was quiet in there. Probably it was taking her time to pack.

Ruth . . . Ruth . . . Ruth. . . .

He remembered that she'd taken his probation report with better balance than the officials. But she was trained in his field and she'd suspected for some time that her father was disturbed. Thurlow remembered he'd gone out to the hospital immediately after the session in the probation office. Ruth had accompanied him, looking withdrawn and fearful, into the almost deserted cafeteria. They'd taken their cups to a corner table. He remembered the steam-table smell of the place, the faint antiseptic background, the marbleized linoleum tabletop with its leftover coffee stains.

Her cup had clattered in a trembling staccato as she'd put it down. He'd sat silently for a moment, sensing her need to come to grips with what he'd told her.

Presently, she'd nodded, then: "I knew it . . . I guess."

"Ruth, I'll do everything I. . . ."

"No." She tucked a strand of red hair under her cap. "They let him call me from the jail . . . just before you came. He was furious with you. He won't accept anything you say."

They must've told him about my report, Thurlow thought. "Now he knows his mask of sanity isn't working," he said. "Of course he's furious."

"Andy . . . are you sure?"

She put her hand on his, her palm damp with perspiration. He held her hand, thinking of mingled perspiration: the idea carried an odd sense of intimacy.

"You're sure," she sighed. "I've seen it coming." Again, that deep sigh. "I didn't tell you about Christmas."

"Christmas?"

"Christmas Eve. My . . . I came home from the hospital. I had the late shift then, remember? He was walking around talking to himself . . . saying horrible things about mother. I could hear her upstairs in her room . . . crying. I . . . I guess I screamed at him, called him a liar."

She took two quick breaths.

"He . . . hit me, knocked me into the Christmas tree . . . everything knocked over . . ." She put a hand to her eyes. "He'd never hit me before—always said he didn't believe in spankings, he'd had so many beatings when he was a boy."

"Why didn't you tell me?"

"We were . . . I . . . I was ashamed of . . . I thought if. . . ." She shrugged. "I went out to the clinic and saw Dr. Whelye, but he said . . . fights, people in the conflict of marriage are. . . ."

"Sounds like him. Did your mother know he hit you?"

"She heard him storm out and slam the door. He didn't come back all night. Christmas Eve! She . . . she'd heard the commotion. She came down, helped me clean up the mess."

"I wish I'd known this when I was talking to. . . ."

"What good would it do? Everyone defends him, even mother. You know what she said while she was helping me clean up? 'Your father's a very sick man, Ruthy.' Defending him!"

"What about your neighbor, Sarah French? Does . . . ?"

"Oh . . . she and Dr. French heard the fights. Sarah . . . Sarah knows daddy's sick. Dr. French . . ." Ruth shrugged.

"But as long as she knows, maybe. . . ."

"She doesn't mean mental illness. Dr. French thinks he has a progressive sclerotic condition, but daddy won't go into the hospital for a complete examination. She knows about that and that's what she meant. That's all she meant!"

"Ruth. . . ." He thought about this revelation for a moment. "Ruth, severe conditions of this kind, Mönckeberg's sclerosis, for example, frequently are accompanied by personality distortions. Didn't you know this?"

"I . . . he wouldn't cooperate, go to a hospital or anything. I talked to Dr. French . . . Whelye. He was no help at all. I warned mother—the violence and. . . ."

"Perhaps if she'd . . . ."

"They've been married twenty-seven years. I can't convince her he really might harm her."

"But he struck you, knocked you down."

"She said I provoked him."

Memories, memories—an antiseptic little corner of the hospital cafeteria and it was fixed in his memory now as indelibly as was this dark street outside the house where Ruth had lived with Nev. The warnings about Joe Murphey had been plain enough, but the world wasn't yet prepared to understand and protect itself from its own madness.

Again, he looked at the silent house, the glow of lights through the rain. As he looked, a woman in a glistening raincoat came running out between Ruth's house and the one on the left. For an instant, he thought it was Ruth and he was half out of the car before the streetlight hit her and he saw it was an older woman with a coat thrown on over a robe. She wore slippers that squished wetly as she crossed the lawn.

"You, there!" she called, waving at Thurlow.

Thurlow came fully out of the car. The rain was cold in his hair, on his face. He felt overcome with foreboding.

The woman came panting up to him, stopped with the rain running down out of her gray hair. "Our telephone's out," she said. "My husband's run across to the Innesses to use theirs, but I thought maybe all the phones're out, so I came. . . ."

"Why do you need a phone?" The words sounded hoarse even to him.

"We live next door. . . ." She pointed. "I can see from our kitchen across the patio to the Hudsons' and I saw him lying there, so I ran over . . . he's dead. . . ."

"Ruth . . . Mrs. Hudson?"

"No, Mr. Hudson. I saw her come in a while ago, but there's no sign of her around. We've got to call the police."

"Yes, yes, of course." He started toward the house.

"She's not in there, I tell you. I ran all through the house."

"Maybe . . . maybe you missed. . . ."

"Mister, there's been a terrible accident, maybe she's already gone for help."

"Accident?" He turned, stared back at her.

"He fell into one of them glass doors, cut an artery, looks like. She probably ran for help."

"But . . . I was out here and. . . ."

A police cruiser came around the corner to his left, its red light flashing. It pulled to a stop behind his car. Two officers got out. Thurlow recognized one of them—Maybeck, Carl Maybeck, a slim angular man with bony wrists, narrow face. He came loping across the lawn to Thurlow while his companion went to the woman.

"Oh . . . Dr. Thurlow," Maybeck said. "Didn't recognize you." He stopped, facing Thurlow. "What's the trouble. We got a call, something about an accident. Ambulance's on the way."

"The woman there . . ." Thurlow nodded toward her, ". . . says Nev Hudson's dead, something about falling into some glass. She may be mistaken. Shouldn't we get inside and. . . ."

"Right away, Doc."

Maybeck led the way running up to the front door. It was locked.

"Around the side," the woman called from behind them. "Patio doors're open."

They ran back down the steps, around the side, wet leaves of shrubbery soaking them. Thurlow felt himself moving in a daze. *Ruth! My God, where are you?* He skidded on the wet bricks of the patio, almost fell, righted himself and was staring down at the red mess that had been Nev Hudson.

Maybeck straightened from a brief examination of the man. "Dead all right." He looked at Thurlow. "How long you been here, Doc?"

"He brought Mrs. Hudson about half an hour ago." It was the neighbor woman. She came to a stop beside Thurlow. "He's dead isn't he?" How delighted she sounded!

"I . . . I've been waiting in the car," Thurlow said.

"That's right," the woman said. "We saw them come up. Expected another fight between Hudson there and his Missus. I heard the crash, him falling, but I was in the bathroom. I came right out to the kitchen."

"Did you see Mrs. Hudson?" Maybeck asked.

"She wasn't anywhere around. There was a lot of smoke coming out these doors here, though. He may've burnt something. He drank a lot, Mr. Hudson. May've been trying to open the doors for the smoke and. . . ." She pointed to the body.

Thurlow wet his lips with his tongue. He was afraid to go in that house, he realized. He said: "Hadn't we better look inside. Perhaps. . . ."

Maybeck met his stare. "Yes. Perhaps we had better."

They could hear an ambulance siren now. It wailed to silence out front. The other officer came around the house, said: "Ambulance is here, Carl. Where. . . ." He saw the body.

"Tell 'em not to disturb any more than they have to," Maybeck said. "We're going to look around inside."

The other officer peered suspiciously at Thurlow.

"This is Dr. Thurlow," Maybeck said.

"Oh." The officer turned to direct men in white coming around the house.

Maybeck led the way inside.

Thurlow was caught immediately by the sight of Ruth's clothing thrown on the bed. His chest felt tight, painful. The neighbor woman had said Ruth wasn't here, but. . . .

Maybeck stooped, peered under the bed. He straightened, sniffed. "You smell something, Doc?"

Thurlow grew aware that there was an odd odor in the room—almost like burnt insulation.

"Almost smells like fire and brimstone," Maybeck said. "Probably *was* something burned in here." He glanced around. There was an empty ashtray on a night stand. It was clean. He looked in the closet, went into an adjoining bath, returned shaking his head.

Thurlow went out to the hall, looked down it toward

the living room. Maybeck brushed past him, led the way into the room. He moved cautiously but with a practiced sureness, peered into the hall closet, behind a davenport. He touched only what he had to touch for his investigation.

They progressed through the house this way, Thurlow a hesitant onlooker, fearful of what they might find around the next corner.

Shortly, they were back in the bedroom.

The ambulance doctor stood in the door, smoking. He glanced at Maybeck. "Not much we can do here, Carl. Coroner's on his way."

"What's it look like?" Maybeck asked. "Was he pushed?"

"Looks like he stumbled," the doctor said. "Carpets pushed up there by his feet. Can't say much about his condition at the time, but there's a smell of whiskey on him."

Maybeck nodded, taking in the evidence. They could hear the other officer talking outside to the neighbor woman. "I don't know what it was." she said, her voice rising. "It just looked like a big cloud of smoke . . , steam, maybe. Or it could've been an insect bomb— something white and smoky."

Thurlow turned his back on the door. He found he couldn't stand the sight of the sprawled body. Ruth wasn't in the house; no doubt of that.*

Insect bomb, he thought. *White and smoky.*

He recalled the grove then, the hovering *something* which Ruth had seen as a cloud. Abruptly, he knew what had happened to her. She wouldn't have disappeared like this without some word to him. *Something* had intruded here and taken her away. It would explain the strange smell, the presence of the thing at the grove, the interest of those weird creatures with their glowing eyes.

But why? he asked himself. *What do they want?*

Then: *This is crazy! She was here when Nev injured himself and she ran for help. She's at a neighbor's and she'll be back any moment.*

And his mind said: *She's been gone a long time.*

She saw the crowd and now she's frightened, he told himself.

There was a bustle of activity at the door behind him—the coroner and the police homicide squad. Maybeck came up beside Thurlow, said: "Doc, they want you to come down to the station and make a statement."

"Yes," he said. "Of course." Then: "That's the homicide detail. Surely they don't think. . . ."

"Just routine, Doc," Maybeck said. "You know that. It looks like he was drinking and stumbled, but Mrs. Hudson's not around. We have to make sure . . . you know."

"I see." He allowed himself to be led out the door past the still figure that had been Ruth's husband, past the men with tape measures and cameras and dusting brushes and coldly measuring eyes.

Ruth's husband . . . Ruth's husband. . . . The label boiled in his mind. *Where is she? Did she break down and run away? But she isn't the type for that. She was under strain, yes, but. . . . What was that cloud the neighbor saw? What was that smell in the room?*

They were outside then. The rain had stopped, but the shrubbery beside the house still drenched them. Porch lights were on across the street. People stood there staring. A white lab truck had been pulled into the driveway beside the house on the other side.

"You know, Doc," Maybeck said. "You really shouldn't drive at night with those dark glasses."

"They're . . . adjustable," Thurlow said. "Not as dark as they look."

Ruth! Where are you?

He wondered then: *Did she push Nev . . . a fight? Did she think people would say, "Like father, like daughter"? Did she run, not wanting to drag me into it?*

"You can ride with us," Maybeck said. "We'll bring you back to your car later."

"Yes." He allowed himself to be eased into the back seat. Then: "Ruth . . . Mrs. Hudson—shouldn't someone be looking for . . ."

"We're looking for her, Doc," Maybeck said. "We'll find her, never you worry."

Will you find her? Thurlow wondered. *What was that thing at the grove—looking at us, trying to manipulate our emotions? It was real. I know it was real. If it wasn't real, then I'm insane. And I know I'm not insane.*

He looked down at his feet in the dim shadows behind the seat. They were soaking from the walk across the wet lawn.

Joe Murphey, he thought. *Joe knows he isn't insane.*

11

RUTH AWOKE ON SOMETHING SOFT—SOOTHING BLUE-gray light. She felt around her: a bed, silky warm covers. She realized she was nude on the bed ... but warm ... warm. Above her there was an oval shape full of glittering crystal facets. They changed colors as she watched—green, silver, yellow, blue. . . . They were soothing.

Somewhere she knew there was something urgently demanding her attention, but it was a paradox. Her whole being told her the urgent thing could wait.

She turned her head to the right. There was light from somewhere, but she couldn't determine its source—a light suddenly full of yellows like remembered sunlight. It illuminated an odd room—a wall lined with what appeared to be books, a low oval table cluttered with strange golden shapes: cubes, rectangular containers, a domed half-egg. There was a window with night's blue blackness pushing against it. As she watched, the window became metallic white and a face appeared there to look in at her. It was a big face, odd silvery skin with harsh angles and planes, the eyes sunken, penetrating.

Ruth felt she should be frightened by that face, but she couldn't find the emotional response.

The face disappeared and the window became a view looking down onto a seashore, surf-battered cliffs, dripping rocks, sunlight. Again, there was night's darkness in the scene and she realized that the framed shape could not be a window.

In front of it stood a wheeled stand holding an unevenly stacked, multibanked shape like a surrealistic typewriter.

A draft touched the left side of her body. It was the first cold thing she had experienced since awakening. She turned toward it, saw an oval door. It stood open, but iris leaves were sinking inward to seal it. Just inside the door stood a squat figure in green leotards—the face that had peered in at her. Somewhere within her there was a reaction which said: *"This is a loathsome, bowlegged little man."* The reaction refused to surface.

The creature's wide, thick-lipped mouth opened. He said: "I am Kelexel." The voice was smooth. It went through her with a tingling sensation.

His eyes traversed her body and she recognized the intense maleness of the look, was surprised to find herself not repelled by it. This room was so warmly soothing, the crystal facets above her moved with such gentle beauty.

"I find you very attractive," Kelexel said. "I do not remember ever being attracted thus, with such magnetism."

He walked around the place where she lay.

Ruth followed him with her eyes, watched him manipulate keys on the machine atop the wheeled stand. A delicious tremor ran through her and she began to wonder what it would be like to have this strange creature, this Kelexel, as a lover.

Distantly within her, she sensed a voice screaming: *'No! No! No!'* Slowly, the voice dimmed, grew silent.

Kelexel came to stand over her.

"I am of the Chem," he said. "Does this mean anything to you?"

She shook her head. "No." Her voice was faint.

"You have not seen a person such as myself before?" Kelexel asked.

"The. . . ." She remembered her last few minutes with Nev, the creatures in the doorway. And Andy. She knew there was something she should feel about Andy Thurlow, a deep and abiding emotion, but there was only a sisterly affection. *Dear Andy . . . such a sweet, dear person.*

"You must answer me," Kelexel said. There was a deep feeling of power in his voice.

"I saw . . . three . . . at my house . . . three who . . ."

"Ah, the three who brought you here," Kelexel said. "But before that, had you seen any of us before that?"

She thought then of the grove, Andy's description (kind, pleasant Andy) but she hadn't really seen such creatures there.

"No," she said.

Kelexel hesitated, glanced at the telltales of the manipulator which controlled the native female's emotions. She was telling the truth. Still, it paid to be cautious.

"Then it means nothing to you that I am of the Chem?" he asked.

"What . . . are the Chem?" she asked. A part of her was aroused now to intense curiosity. The curiosity struggled up through muddy waves of distraction to sit in her awareness and stare at Kelexel. What a gnome of a creature! What a sweet little gnome.

"It shall mean something," Kelexel said. "You are very attractive to me. We Chem are kind to those who please us. You cannot go back to your friends, of course, not ever. There are compensations, however. It's considered an honor to serve the Chem."

Where is Andy? Ruth wondered. *Dear, sweet Andy.*

"Very attractive," Kelexel murmured.

Wondering at the force which moved him, Kelexel extended a knob-knuckled finger, touched her right breast. How resilient and lovely her skin. The finger moved gently up to the nipple, to her neck, her chin, her lips, her hair.

"Your eyes are green," Kelexel said. "We Chem are very fond of green."

Ruth swallowed. The caressing movement of Kelexel's finger filled her with excitement. His face dominated her vision. She reached up, touched his hand. How hard and virile the hand felt. She met the penetrating stare of his brown eyes.

The manipulator's instruments told Kelexel that the female was now completely subjugated to his will. The realization stirred him. He smiled, exposing square silvery teeth. "I will have many questions for you," he said. "Later."

Ruth felt herself sinking into a golden daze. Her attention was locked onto the crystal facets glittering above the bed. Kelexel's head momentarily obscured the kaleidoscopic movement, then she felt his face pressed between her breasts. The golden daze overwhelmed her with ripples and waves of terrifying ecstasy.

"Oh, God," she whispered. "Oh, God. Oh, God."

How pleasant to be worshiped at such a moment, Kelexel thought. It was the most pleasure he had ever experienced from a female.

12

RUTH WAS TO LOOK BACK AT THE FIRST FEW CHEM days with a profound astonishment at herself. She grew aware (slowly) that Kelexel was twisting her responses with his outlandish devices, but by that time she was addicted to the manipulation. It was only important that Kelexel return to touch her and speak to her and twist her to his desires.

He grew handsome in her sight. It gave her pleasure just to look at his ridged, tubular body. His square face was easy to read in his devotion to her.

He really loves me, she thought. *He had Nev killed to get me.*

There was even pleasure in the realization of how utterly helpless she was, how completely subject to Kelexel's slightest whim. She had come to understand by then that the most powerful force on earth was as an ant hill when compared to the Chem. By this time she'd been through an educational imprinter, spoke Chem and shiptongue.

The major irritant in her existence at this moment was remembrance of Andy Thurlow. Kelexel had begun to ease back on the strength of the manipulator (her reactions were now sufficiently conditioned) and she could remember Andy with growing clarity. But the fact of her helplessness eased her guilt feelings, and Andy came less and less into her thoughts until Kelexel brought her a pantovive.

Kelexel had learned his lesson with the Subi creature. *Activity slows the aging process of a mortal*, he reminded himself, and he had Ynvic fit Ruth to a pantovive with access to the storyship's Archive Storage system.

The machine was introduced into a corner of her prison-room, a room that already had taken on touches of her personality as Kelexel fitted it to her wishes. A complete bathroom-dressing room had been installed adjoining it. Clothing? She had but to ask, Kelexel filled a closet to overflowing. Jewelry, perfumes, choice foods: all came at her bidding.

Kelexel bent to every request, knowing himself to be besotted with her and enjoying every moment of it. When he caught the crewmen exchanging sly looks he smiled to himself. They must all have their pleasure creatures from this planet. He presumed that the native males must be just as exciting to Chem females; it was one of the attractions of the place, one of the reasons Fraffin had been so successful here.

Thoughts of his purpose here, his duty, slipped temporarily into the background. He knew the Primacy would understand when he explained and displayed his pleasure creature. After all, what was Time to a Chem? The Investigation would continue, merely a bit slowed . . . temporarily.

At first, the pantovive frightened Ruth. She shook her head as Kelexel tried to explain its purpose and workings. How it worked; that was easy enough to understand. Why it worked was completely beyond her comprehension.

It was the time she had come to call afternoon, although there was little sense of day and night here in the ship. Afternoon merely meant that Kelexel had come from whatever mysterious duties took him away and he would now spend a relaxation and rest period with her. Ruth sat in the fitted contours of the control chair. The room's lights were tuned to muted yellow and the pantovive filled her attention.

The thing somewhat fitted her ideas of a machine. The chair nestled part way into it. There were control rings in the chair arms, banks of knobs and keys to left and right, rows of them in coded colors—yellows, reds, grays, blacks, greens, blues, a series of orange and white ones looking like a crazy piano. Directly in front and slightly below her extended an oval platform with shimmering lines extending to it from behind the banks of keys.

Kelexel stood behind her, a hand on her shoulder. He felt a rather distant pride showing the wonders of Chem civilization to his new pet . . . his lovely new pet.

"Use voice or key command to select the period and title you wish," he said. "Just as you heard me do. This unit is keyed to your tongue or Chem and will accept and translate in that mode. This is an editing pantovive and looks complicated, but you may ignore most of the controls. They're not connected. Remember, you first open the channel to Archives by depressing this key." He demonstrated, pushing an orange key on her right. "Once you've selected your story, lock it in thusly." Again, he demonstrated. "Now, you can begin the action." He depressed a white key at far left.

A mob, its figures reduced to quarter size, formed on the oval stage in front of her. A sense of mad excitement radiated from them through the sensi-mesh circuits. She sat bolt upright as the emotion swept over her.

"You're feeling the emotion of the creatures on the stage," Kelexel said. "If it's too strong, reduce it by turning this control to your left." He moved a dial on the chair arm. The excitement ebbed.

"Is it real?" she asked.

The mob was a wash of colors in antique styles—blues, flutters of red, dirty rags on arms and feet, rare glitters of buttons or emblems, tricorne hats on some of the men, red cockades. There was an odd familiarity about the scene that inflicted Ruth with an abrupt feeling of fear. Her body came alive to tom-tom pulsebeats from some fire-flickering past. She sensed driving rhythms of drums within herself.

"Is it real?" she demanded, raising her voice this time.

The mob was running now, feet thudding. Brown feet winked under the long dresses of the women.

"Real?" Kelexel asked. "What an odd question. It's . . . perhaps real in a sense. It happened to natives such as yourself. Real—how strange. That idea has never concerned me."

The mob ran through a park now. Kelexel bent over Ruth's shoulder, sharing the aura of the sensi-mesh web. There came a wet smell of grass, evergreens with their resin pungency, the sweaty stink of the natives in their exertions. Stage center focused down onto the running legs. They rushed past with a scissoring urgency, across brown paths, grass, disturbing yellow petals in a flower border. Wet wind, busy feet, crushed petals—there was fascination in the movement.

Viewpoint drew back, back, back. A cobbled street, high stone walls came into stage center. The mob raced toward the gray stained walls. Steel flashed in their midst now.

"They appear to be storming a citadel," Kelexel said.

"The Bastille," Ruth whispered. "It's the Bastille."

The recognition held her hypnotized. Here was the actual storming of the Bastille. No matter the present date, here in front of her senses it was July 14, 1789, with an organized movement of soldiery sweeping in from the right of the mob. There was the clatter of hooves on stone, gun carriages rumbling, hoarse shouts, curses. The pantovive's translator rendered them faithfully into English because she had asked for it in English.

Ruth gripped the arms of her chair.

Abruptly, Kelexel reached forward, depressed a gray key at her left. The scene faded.

"I remember that one well," he said. "One of Fraffin's more successful productions." He touched Ruth's hair. "You understand how it works now? Focusing here." His hand came forward, demonstrating. "Intensity here. It's quite simple to operate and should provide you many hours of enjoyment."

Enjoyment? Ruth thought.

Slowly, she turned, looked up at Kelexel. There was a lost sense of horror in her eyes. *The storming of the Bastille: a Fraffin production!*

Fraffin's name was known to her. Kelexel had explained the workings of the storyship.

Storyship!

Until this moment, she hadn't begun to plumb the implications behind that label.

Storyship.

"Duties call me elsewhere at the moment," Kelexel said. "I'll leave you to the enjoyment of your pantovive."

"I . . . thought you were going to . . . stay," she said. Suddenly, she didn't want to be alone with this machine. She recognized it as an attractive horror, a thing of creative reality that might open a hoard of locked things which she couldn't face. She felt that the reality of the pantovive might turn into flames and scorch her. It was wild, potent, dangerous and she could never control it nor chain her own desires to use it.

Ruth took Kelexel's hand, forced a smile onto her face. "Please stay."

Kelexel hesitated. The invitation in his pet's face was obvious and attractive, but Ynvic, fitting Ruth to the pantovive, had sent a new train of ideas coursing through his mind. He felt the stirrings of responsibility, his duty to the Investigation. Ynvic, the oddly stolid and laconic shipsurgeon, yes—she might just be the weak spot in Fraffin's organization. Kelexel felt the need to test this new avenue.

"I'm sorry," he said, "but I must leave. I'll return as soon as possible."

She saw she couldn't move him and she dropped back, faced the raw temptation which was this machine. There came the sounds of Kelexel leaving and she was alone with the pantovive.

Presently, she said: "Current story in progress, latest production." She depressed the proper keys.

The oval stage grew almost dark with little star glimmers of yellow along its edges. A dot of blue light appeared at the center of focus, flickered, washed white and suddenly there was a man standing at a mirror shaving with a straightedge razor. She gasped with recognition. It was Anthony Bondelli, her father's attorney. She held her breath, trying to still a terrifying sense of eavesdropping.

Bondelli stood with his back to her, his face visible

as a reflection in the mirror. It was a deeply tanned
face with two wings of smooth black hair sweeping
back from a high, thin forehead. His nostrils flared
above a pencil-line mustache and small mouth. The
chin was broad, out of proportion with the narrow
features, a fact she had noted before. He radiated a
feeling of sleepy complacency.

And indistinct shouting began to dominate the scene.
Bondelli paused in his shaving, turned and called
through an open doorway on his right: "What th' hell's
all that noise?" He resumed shaving, muttered: "Always turn that damn' TV too loud."

Ruth grew conscious of odors in the scene—a wet
smell of shaving soap and over that the pervasive
aroma of frying bacon. The realism held her rigid in
her chair. She felt herself breathing quietly lest Bondelli turn and find her spying.

Presently, a woman in a bold Chinese-pattern
dressing gown appeared in the bathroom doorway. She
held her hands rigidly clasped in front of her bosom:

In a sudden premonition, Ruth wanted to turn off
the pantovive, but her muscles refused to obey. She
knew the woman in the dressing gown: Marge Bondelli,
a pleasantly familiar figure with braided blonde hair
pinned back from her round face. That face was con-
torted now in shock.

"Tony!" she said.

Bondelli pulled the razor slowly down beneath his
jaw, taking care at the pattern of deep creases which
ran from the sides of his jaw down along his neck.
"Whuzzit?"

The television still could be heard in the background, a muted sense of conversation. Bondelli pulled
the razor slowly upward. A look of glazed shock dominated his wife's blue eyes. She said: "Joe Murphey
killed Adele last night!"

"Ouch!" A thin line of red appeared on Bondelli's
neck. He ignored it, splashed the razor down into the
washbasin, whirled.

Ruth felt herself trembling uncontrollably. *It's just
like a movie*, she told herself. *This isn't really happen-*

ing right now. Pain in her chest made it difficult to breathe. *My mother's death is a Fraffin Production!*

"That terrible sword," Bondelli's wife whispered.

Bondelli thrust himself away from the washbasin, passed his wife, went into the living room and stood before the television.

Ruth felt herself drawn into his wake, a participant, sharing the horror and shock which radiated from the Bondellis as the pantovive amplified her own emotions. The television announcer was recapping the story, using still photographs taken by the town's own newspaper photographer. Ruth stared at the photographs—her mother's face, her father's . . . diagrams with white X's and arrows. She willed herself to turn away from this horror, could not move.

Bondelli said: "Never mind my breakfast. I'm going down to the office."

"You're bleeding," his wife said. She had brought a styptic pencil from the bathroom. She dabbed at the cut on his neck. "Hold still. It'll get all over your collar." She pushed up his chin. "Tony . . . you stay out of this. You're not a criminal lawyer."

"But I've handled Joe's law ever since he. . . . Ouch! Damn it, Marge, that stings!"

"Well, you can't go out bleeding like that," She finished, put the pencil beside the washbasin. "Tony, I've a funny feeling . . . don't get involved."

"I'm Joe's lawyer. I'm already involved."

Abruptly, Ruth found control of her muscles. She slapped the pantovive shutoff, leaped to her feet, pushing herself away from the machine.

My mother's murder something to amuse the Chem!

She whirled away, strode toward the bed. The bed repelled her. She turned her back on it. The casual way Kelexel had left her to discover this filled her with terrified anger. Surely he must've known she'd find out. He didn't care! No, it was worse than that: he hadn't even thought about it. The whole thing was of no concern to him. It was beneath his attention. It was less than not caring. It was disdain, repellant . . . hateful. . . .

Ruth looked down, found she was wringing her

hands. She glanced around the room. There must be some weapon here, anything with which to attack that hideous. . . . Again, she saw the bed. She thought of the golden ecstasy there and suddenly hated her own body. She wanted to tear her flesh. Tears started from her eyes. She strode back and forth, back and forth.

I'll kill him!

But Kelexel had said the Chem were immune to personal violence. They were immortal. They couldn't be killed. They never died.

The thought made her feel like an infinitesimal mote, a dust speck, lost, alone, doomed. She threw herself onto the bed, turned onto her back and stared up at the crystal glittering of the machine which she knew Kelexel used to control her. There was a link to it under his cloak. She'd seen him working it.

Thought of the machine filled her with an agony of prescience: she knew what she would do when Kelexel returned. She would succumb to him once more. The golden ecstasy would overcome her senses. She would end by fawning on him, begging for his attentions.

"Oh, God!" she whispered.

She turned, stared at the pantovive. That machine would contain the entire record of her mother's death—she knew it. The actual scene was there. She wondered then if she would have the strength to resist asking for that scene.

Something hissed behind her and she whirled on the bed, stared at the door.

Ynvic stood just inside, her bald head glistening in the yellow light. Ruth glared at the gnome figure, the bulge of breasts, the stocky legs in green leotards.

"You are troubled," Ynvic said. Her voice was professionally smooth, soothing. It sounded like the voices of so many doctors she had heard that Ruth wanted to cry out.

"What're you doing here?" Ruth asked.

"I am shipsurgeon," Ynvic said. "Most of my job is just being available. You have need of me."

They look like caricatures of human beings, Ruth thought.

"Go away," she said.

"You have problems and I can help you," Yvnic said.

Ruth sat up. "Problems? Why would I have problems?" She knew her voice sounded hysterical.

"That fool Kelexel left you with an unrestricted pantovive," Ynvic said.

Ruth studied the Chem female. Did they have emotions? Was there any way to touch them, hurt them? Even to cause them a pinprick of pain seemed the most desirable thing in the universe.

"How do you ugly creatures breed?" Ruth asked.

"You hate us, eh?" Ynvic asked.

"Are you afraid to answer?" Ruth demanded.

Ynvic shrugged. "Essentially, it's the same as with your kind . . . except that females are deprived of the reproductive organs at an early stage in their development. We must go to breeding centers, get permission—it's a very tiresome, boring procedure. We manage to enjoy ourselves quite well without the organs." She advanced to stand a pace from the bed.

"But your men prefer my kind," Ruth said.

Again, Ynvic shrugged. "Tastes differ. I've had lovers from your planet. Some of them were good, some weren't. The trouble is, you fade so quickly."

"But you enjoy us! We amuse you!"

"Up to a point," Ynvic said. "Interest waxes and wanes."

"Then why do you stay here?"

"It's profitable," Ynvic said. And she noted that the native female already was coming out of the emotional spiral that had trapped her. Resistance, an object to hate—that's all it took. The creatures were so easy to maneuver.

"So the Chem like us," Ruth said. "They like stories about us."

"You're an endless pot of self-generating stories," Ynvic said. "All by yourselves you can produce natural sequences of true artistic merit. This is, of course, at once a profound source of frustration and requires very delicate handling to capture and reproduce for our audiences. Fraffin's art rests in eliciting those subtle nuances which prick our risibilities, capture our fascinated attention."

"You disgust me," Ruth hissed. "You're not human."

"We're not mortal," Ynvic said. And she thought: *I wonder if the creature's already with child? What'll she do when she learns she'll bear a Chem?*

"But you hide from us," Ruth said. She pointed at the ceiling. "Up there."

"When it suits our purpose," Ynvic said. "We are required to stay concealed now, of course. But it wasn't always that way. I've lived openly with your kind."

Ruth found herself caught by the casual aloofness in Ynvic's tone. She knew she couldn't hurt this creature, but had to try.

"You're lying," Ruth said.

"Perhaps. But I'll tell you that I once was the God Ea, striking terror into captive Jews ... in Sumeria a while back. It was harmless fun setting up religious patterns among you."

"You posed as a god?" Ruth shuddered. She knew the words were true. They were spoken with too little effort. They meant so little to the speaker.

"I've also been a circus freak," Ynvic said. "I've worked in many epics. Sometimes I enjoy the illusion of antiquity."

Ruth shook her head, unable to speak.

"You don't understand," Ynvic said. "How could you? It's *our* problem, you see? When the future's infinite, you have no antiquities. You're always caught up in the Forever-Now. When you think you've come to terms with the fact that your past is unimportant, then the future becomes unimportant. That can be fatal. The storyships protect us from this fatality."

"You ... spy on us for. . . ."

"Infinite past, infinite future, infinte present," Ynvic said. She bent her head, liking the sound of the words. "Yes, we have these. Your lives are but brief bursts and your entire past little more—yet we Chem gain from you the explicit feeling of something ancient ... an important past. You give us this, do you understand?"

Again, Ruth shook her head. The words seemed to

have meaning, but she felt she was getting only part of their sense.

"It's something we can't get from Tiggywaugh's web," Ynvic said. "Perhaps it's something our immortality denies us. The web makes the Chem into one organism—I can feel the life of each of the others, billions upon billions of Chem. This is ... old, but it's not ancient."

Ruth swallowed. The creature was rambling. But the conversation was providing a time to recover, and Ruth felt forming within her a place of resistance, a core place where she could retreat and in which she was safe from the Chem ... no matter what they did to her. She knew she'd succumb to Kelexel still, that this Ynvic creature even now was doing something to shade the Chem captive's emotional responses. But the core place was there, growing, imparting purpose.

"No matter," Ynvic said. "I've come to examine you." She advanced to the edge of the bed.

Ruth inhaled a deep, trembling breath. "You were watching me," she said. "At the machine. Does Kelexel know?"

Ynvic became very still. How did the stupid native know to ask such a penetrating question?

Ruth sensed the opening in Ynvic's guard, said: "You speak of infinity, of epics, but you use your ... whatever ..." She made a sweeping gesture to take in the storyship ". . . to . . . record a . . . killing. . . ."

"Indeed!" Ynvic said. "You will tell me now why Kelexel is asking for me out in the ship."

The crystal facets above the bed began emitting a blue glow. Ruth felt her will melting. She shook her head. "I . . . don't. . . ."

"You will tell me!" The Chem female's face was a round mask of fury, the bald head glistening wetly silver.

"I . . . don't . . . know," Ruth whispered.

"He was a fool to give you an unrestricted pantovive and we were fools to go along with it," Ynvic said. She passed a hand across her thick lips. "What do you understand of such things?"

Ruth felt the pressure relaxing, took a deep breath. The core place of retreat was still there. "It was my mother, my mother you killed," she muttered.

"We killed?"

"You make people do what you want them to do," Ruth said.

"People!" Ynvic sneered. Ruth's answers betrayed only the shallowest knowledge of Chem affairs. There was danger in the creature, though. She might yet excite Kelexel's interests into the wrong paths too soon.

Ynvic put a hand on Ruth's abdomen, glanced at the manipulator over the bed. The pattern of the lambent blue glow shifted in a way that made her smile. This poor creature already was impregnated. What a strange way to bear offspring! But how lovely and subtle a way to trap a snooper from the Primacy.

The fact of Ruth's pregnancy imparted an odd feeling of disquiet to Ynvic. She withdrew her hand, grew aware of the characteristic musky scent of the native female. What gross mammary glands the creature had! Yet, her cheeks were indrawn as though from undernourishment. She wore a loose flowing gown that reminded Ynvic of Grecian garments. Now there'd been an interesting culture, but brief, so brief . . . everything so brief.

But she's pregnant, Ynvic thought, *I should be delighted. Why does it bother me? What have I overlooked?*

For no reason she could explain, four lines from a Chem drinking song poured through Ynvic's mind then—

> *"In the long-long-long ago*
> *When each of us was young,*
> *We heard the music of the flesh*
> *And the singing of a sun . . ."*

Ynvic shook her head sharply. The song was meaningless. It was good only for its rhythms, a plaything series of noises, another toy.

But what had it meant . . . once?

Over the bed, the manipulator's lenses sank back through green and stopped in a soft pastel red.

"Rest, little innocent," Ynvic said. She placed a strangely gentle hand on Ruth's bare arm. "Rest and be attractive for Kelexel's return."

13

"THE SIMPLE TRUTH OF THE MATTER IS THAT THINGS got too much for her and she ran away," Bondelli said. He stared across at Andy Thurlow, wondering at the odd, haggard look of the man.

They sat in Bondelli's law office, a place of polished wood and leather-bound books aligned precisely behind glass covers, a place of framed diplomas and autographed photos of important people. It was early afternoon, a sunny day.

Thurlow was bent over, elbows on knees, hands clasped tightly together. *I don't dare tell him my real suspicions,* he thought. *I don't dare . . . I don't dare.*

"Who'd want to harm her or take her away?" Bondelli asked. "She's gone to friends, perhaps up in 'Frisco. It's something simple as that. We'll hear from her when she's gotten over her funk."

"That's what the police think," Thurlow said. "They've completely cleared her of any complicity in Nev's death . . . the physical evidence. . . ."

"Then the best thing we can do is get down to the necessities of Joe's case. Ruth'll come home when she's ready."

Will she? Thurlow asked himself. He couldn't shake off the feeling that he was living in a nightmare. Had he really been with Ruth at the grove? Was Nev really dead in that weird accident? Had Ruth run off? If so, where?

"We're going to have to dive directly into the legal definition of insanity," Bondelli said. "Nature and consequences. Justice requires. . . ."

"Justice?" Thurlow stared at the man. Bondelli had

99

turned in his chair, revealing his profile, the mouth thinned to a shadowline beneath the mustache.

"Justice," Bondelli repeated. He swiveled to look at Thurlow. Bondelli prided himself upon his judgment of men and he studied Thurlow now. The psychologist appeared to be coming out of his blue funk. No question why the man was so shaken, of course. Still in love with Ruth Murphey . . . Hudson. Terrible mess, but it'd shake down. Always did. That was one thing you learned from the law; it all came out in court.

Thurlow took a deep breath, reminded himself that Bondelli wasn't a criminal lawyer. "We ought to be more interested in realism," he said. There was an undertone of wry cynicism in his voice. *Justice!* "This legal definition of insanity business is a lot of crap. The important thing is that the community wants the man executed—and our benighted D.A., Mr. Paret, is running for reelection."

Bondelli was shocked. "The law's above that!" He shook his head. "And the whole community isn't against Joe. Why should they be?"

Thurlow spoke as though to an unruly child: "Because they're afraid of him, naturally."

Bondelli permitted himself a glance out the window beside his desk—familiar rooftops, distant greenery, a bit of foggy smoke beginning to cloud the air above the adjoining building: The smoke curled and swirled, creating an interesting pattern against the view. He returned his attention to Thurlow, said: "The question is, how can an insane man know the nature and consequences of his act? What I want from you is to explode that nature and consequences thing."

Thurlow removed his glasses, glances at them, returned them to his nose. They made the shadows stand out sharply in the room. "An insane man doesn't think about consequences," he said. And he wondered if he was really going to let himself take part in Bondelli's mad plan for defense of Joe Murphey.

"I'm taking the position," Bondelli said, "that the original views of Lord Cottenham support our defense." Bondelli turned, pulled a thick book out of a cabinet behind him, put the book on the desk and opened it to a marker.

He can't be serious, Thurlow thought.

"Here's Lord Cottenham," Bondelli said. " 'It is wrong to listen to any doctrine which proposes the punishment of persons laboring under insane delusions. It is inconceivable that the man who was incapable of judging between right and wrong, of knowing whether an act were good or bad, ought to be made accountable for his actions; such a man has not that within him which forms the foundation of accountability, either from a moral or a legal point of view. I consider it strange that any person should labor under a delusion and yet be aware that it was a delusion: in fact, if he were aware of his state, which could be no delusion.' "

Bondelli closed the book with a snap, stared at Thurlow as though to say: *"There! It's all solved!"*

Thurlow cleared his throat. It was increasingly obvious that Bondelli lived in a cloud world. "That's all very true, of course," Thurlow said. "But isn't it possible that even if our esteemed district attorney suspects —or even *believes*—Joe Murphey to be insane, he'll think it better to execute such a man than to put him in an institution?"

"Good heavens! Why?"

"The doors of mental hospitals sometimes open," Thurlow said. "Paret was elected to protect this community—even from itself."

"But Murphey's obviously insane!"

"You aren't listening to me," Thurlow said. "Certainly he's insane. That's what people are afraid of."

"But shouldn't psychology. . . ."

"Psychology!" Thurlow snapped.

Bondelli stared at Thurlow in shocked silence.

"Psychology's just the modern superstition," Thurlow said. "It can't do a damned thing for people like Joe. I'm sorry but that's the truth and it'll hurt less to have that out right now."

"If this is what you told Ruth Murphey, no wonder she ran away," Bondelli said.

"I told Ruth I'd help any way I can."

"You have a strange way of showing it."

"Look," Thurlow said. "We've a community up in arms, fearful, excited. Murphey's the focus for their hidden guilt feelings. They want him dead. They want this psycological pressure taken off them. You can't psychoanalyze a whole community."

Bondelli began tapping a finger impatiently on the desk. "Will you or will you not help me prove Joe's insane?"

"I'll do everything I can, but you know Joe's going to resist that form of defense, don't you?"

"Know it!" Bondelli leaned forward, arms on his desk. "The damn' fool blows his top at the slightest hint I want him to plead insanity. He keeps harping on the unwritten law!"

"Those stupid accusations against Adele," Thurlow said. "Joe's going to make it very difficult to prove him insane."

"A sane man would fake insanity now if only to save his life," Bondelli said.

"Keep that very clearly in mind," Thurlow said. "Joe can't in any way entertain the idea that he's insane. To admit that—even as a possibility—or as a necessary pretense, he'd have to face the fact that his violent act could've been a useless, senseless thing. The enormity of such an admission would be far worse than insanity. Insanity's much preferable."

"Can you get that across to a jury?" Bondelli asked. He spoke in a hushed tone.

"That Murphey considers it safer to play sane?"

"Yes."

Thurlow shrugged. "Who knows what a jury will believe? Joe may be a hollow shell, but that's one helluva strong shell. Nothing contradictory can be permitted to enter it. Every fiber of him is concentrated on the necessity to appear normal, to maintain the illusion of sanity—for himself as well as for others. Death is far preferable to that other admission . . . Oscar Wilde concurring."

"'Each man kills the thing he loves,'" Bondelli whispered. Again, he turned, looked out the window. The smoky pattern was still there. He wondered idly if workmen were tarring a roof somewhere below him.

Thurlow looked down at Bondelli's tapping finger. "The trouble with you, Tony," he said, "is you're one of G. K. Chesterton's terrible children. You're innocent and love justice. Most of us are wicked and naturally prefer mercy."

As though he hadn't heard, Bondelli said: "We need something simple and elegant to show the jury. They have to be dumbfounded with the realization that. . . ." He broke off, stared at Thurlow. "And your prediction of Joe's trouble fits the bill precisely."

"Too technical," Thurlow said. "A jury won't sit still for it, won't understand it. Juries don't hear what they don't understand. Their minds wander. They think about dress patterns, bugs in the rose garden, what's for lunch, where to spend a vacation."

"You did predict it, didn't you? Ruth did report your words correctly?"

"The psychotic break, yes, I predicted it." The words were almost a sigh. "Tony, haven't you focused on what I've been telling you? This was a sex crime—the sword, the violence. . . ."

"Is he insane?"

"Of course he's insane!"

"In the legal sense?"

"In every sense."

"Well, then there's legal precedent for. . . ."

"Psychological precedent's more important."

"What?"

"Tony, if there's one thing I've learned since becoming court psychologist here, it's that juries spend far more energy trying to discover the judge's opinion than they do following what the opposing lawyers are presenting. Juries have a purely disgusting respect for the wisdom of judges. Any judge we get is going to be a member of this community. The community wants Joe put away permanently—dead. We can prove him insane until we're blue in the face. None of these good people will face our proof consciously, even while they're accepting it unconsciously. In fact, as we prove Joe insane, we're condemning him."

"Are you trying to tell me you can't get up on that stand and say you predicted Joe's insanity but the authorities refused to act because the man was too important a member of the community?"

"Of course I can't."

"You think they won't believe you?"

"It doesn't make any difference whether they believe me!"

"But if they believe. . . ."

"I'll tell you what they'll believe, Tony, and I'm surprised that you, an attorney, don't realize this. They'll believe that Paret has proof of Adele's unfaithfulness, but that some legal technicality, legal trickery on your part, prohibits introduction of the dirty details. They'll believe this because it's the easiest thing to believe. No grandstand play on my part will change that."

"You're saying we don't stand a chance?"

Thurlow shrugged. "Not if it goes to trial right away. If you can delay the trial or get a change of venue. . . ."

Bondelli swiveled his chair, stared through the smoke pattern outside his window. "I find it very hard to believe that reasonable, logical human beings. . . ."

"What's reasonable or logical about a jury?" Thurlow asked.

A flush of anger began at Bondelli's collar, spread upward across his cheeks, into his hair. He turned, glared at Thurlow. "Do you know what I think, Andy? I think the fact that Ruth ran out on you has colored your attitude toward her father. You say you'll help, but every word you. . . ."

"That'll be enough of that," Thurlow interrupted, his voice low, flat. He took two deep breaths. "Tell me something, Tony. Why're you taking this case? You're not a criminal lawyer."

Bondelli passed a hand across his eyes. Slowly, the flush left his skin. He glanced at Thurlow. "Sorry, Andy."

"That's all right. Can you answer the question? Do you know why you're taking this case?"

Bondelli sighed, shrugged. "When the story broke that I was representing him, two of my most important clients called and said they'd take their business elsewhere if I didn't pull out."

"That's why you're defending Joe?"

"He has to have the best defense possible."

"You're the best?"

"I wanted to go up to San Francisco, get Belli or someone of that stature, but Joe refuses. He thinks it's going to be easy—the goddamn' unwritten law."

"And that leaves you."

"In this city, yes." Bondelli extended his arms onto the desk, clasped his hands into fists. "You know, I don't see the problem the same way you do, not at all. I think our biggest job's to prove he isn't faking insanity."

Thurlow took off his glasses, rubbed his eyes. They were beginning to ache. He'd been reading too much today, he thought. He said: "Well, you have a point there, Tony. If a person with delusions learns to keep quiet about them, you can have one helluva time getting him to act on those delusions where people will see him and understand. Exposing faked insanity is easy compared with the problems of detecting a concealed psychosis, but the public generally doesn't understand this."

"I see a four-pronged attack," Bondelli said. "There're four common essentials with insane killers."

Thurlow started to say something, thought better of it as Bondelli raised a hand, four fingers extended.

"First," Bondelli said, "did the victim's death profit the killer. Psychopaths usually kill strangers or persons close to them. You see, I've been doing my homework in your field, too."

"I see that," Thurlow said.

"And Adele had no insurance," Bondelli said. He lowered one finger. "Next, was the murder carefully planned?" Another finger came down. "Psychopaths don't plan their crimes. Either they leave escape to chance, or they make it ridiculously easy for the police to catch them. Joe practically advertised his presence in that office."

Thurlow nodded and began to wonder if Bondelli could be right. *Am I unconsciously attacking Ruth through her father? Where the hell did she go?*

"Third," Bondelli said, "was a great deal more violence than necessary used in the crime? Deranged people continue an attack beyond all reason. There's no doubt the first thrust of that sword would've killed Adele." A third finger came down.

Thurlow returned his glasses to his nose, stared at Bondelli. The attorney was so intent, so sure of himself. Was it possible?

"Fourth," Bondelli said, "was the killing accomplished with an improvised weapon? Persons who plan set themselves up with a lethal weapon beforehand. A psychopath grabs anything at hand—a cleaver, a club, a rock, a piece of furniture." The fourth finger came down and Bondelli lowered a fist to the desk. "That damned sword hung on Joe's study wall for as long as I can remember."

"It all sounds so easy," Thurlow said. "But what's the prosecution gong to be doing all this time?"

"Oh, they'll have their experts, naturally."

"Whelye among them," Thurlow said.

"Your boss at the hospital?"

"The same."

"Does . . . that put you . . . on a spot?"

"That doesn't bother me, Tony. He's just another part of the community syndrome. It's . . . it's the whole mad mess." Thurlow looked down at his hands. "People are going to say Joe's better off dead—even if he is insane. And the prosecution experts you kiss off with a wave of the hand, they're going to be saying things the community *wants* to hear. Everything the judge says is likely to be interpreted. . . ."

"I'm sure we can get an impartial judge."

"Yes . . . no doubt. But judges invariably say the question to be determined is whether at the time of the crime the accused had not the use of that part of his understanding which allowed him to know he was doing a wrong and wicked act. That *part,* Tony; as though the mind could be divided into compartments, part of it sane, part insane. Impossible! The mind's a unified thing. A person can't be mentally and emotionally diseased in some fictitious part without infecting the total personality. A knowledge of right and wrong—the ability to choose between God and the devil—is profoundly different from the knowledge that two plus two equals four. To make the judgment of good and evil requires an intact personality."

Thurlow looked up, studied Bondelli.

The attorney was staring out the window, lips pursed in thought. He obviously hadn't been listening.

Thurlow turned toward the window. He felt sick with frustration and despair, Ruth *had* run away. That was the only logical, sane, reasonable explanation. Her father was doomed, no matter. . . . Thurlow's muscles locked into frozen, glaring suspense. He stared out the window.

Some ten feet out, poised in the air, hovering, was an object . . . a dome-shaped object with a neat round opening that faced Bondelli's window. Behind the opening, figures moved.

Thurlow opened his mouth to speak, found he had no voice. He lurched out of his chair, groped his way around the desk away from the window.

"Andy, is something wrong?" Bondelli asked. The attorney swiveled back, stared up at Thurlow.

Thurlow leaned on the desk facing the window. He looked right into the round opening in the hovering object. There were eyes inside, glowing eyes. A slender tube protruded from the opening. Painful, constricting force pressed in on Thurlow's chest. He had to fight for each breath.

My God! They're trying to kill me! he thought.

Waves of unconsciousness surged over his mind, receded, returned. His chest was a great gasping region of fire. Dimly, he saw the edge of the desk surge upward past his eyes. Something hit a carpeted floor and he realized with fading consciousness that it was his head. He tried to push himself up, collapsed.

"Andy! Andy! What's wrong? Andy!" It was Bondelli's voice. The voice bounced and receded in a wavering, ringing echo box. "Andy . . . Andy . . . And. . . ."

Bondelli stood up from a quick examination of Thurlow, shouted for his secretary: "Mrs. Wilson! Call an ambulance! I think Dr. Thurlow's had a heart attack."

14

I MUST NOT GROW TO LIKE THIS LIFE, KELEXEL TOLD himself. *I have a new pet, yes, but I also have a duty. A moment will come when I must leave, taking my pet, abandoning all the other pleasures of this place.*

He sat in Ruth's private quarters, a bowl of native liquor on a low table between them. Ruth appeared oddly pensive, quiet. The manipulator had required quite heavy pressure to bring her into a responsive mood. This bothered Kelexel. She had been coming along so nicely, taking the training with an ease which delighted him. Now—relapse . . . and just after he had given her such a pleasant toy, the pantovive.

There were fresh flowers on the table beside the liquor. Roses, they were called. Red roses. The liquor had been sent along by Ynvic. Its aroma, a touch on the palate, surprised and delighted Kelexel. Subtle esthers danced on his tongue. The heady central substance required constant readjustment of his metabolism. He wondered how Ruth adapted to the stuff. She was taking an inordinate amount of it.

In spite of the distracting effort at keeping his metabolism in balance, Kelexel found the total experience pleasant. The senses came alert: boredom retreated.

Ynvic had said the liquor was a wine from a sunny valley ". . . up there east of us." It was a native product, lovely stuff.

Kelexel looked up at the silvery gray curve of ceiling, noted the gravity anomaly lines like golden chords above the manipulator. The room was taking on a pleasant air of familiarity with its new touches denoting occupancy by his delightful pet.

"Have you noticed how many of the ship people wear native clothing?" Kelexel asked.

"How could I?" Ruth asked. (How fuzzy her voice sounded.) "When do I ever get out of here?"

"Yes, of course," Kelexel agreed. "I was thinking I might try some of your clothing myself. Ynvic tells me that the garments of some of your larger children often fit the Chem with very slight alteration. Ynvic calls that a fringe benefit."

Ruth refilled her glass from the wine bowl, drank deeply.

The little pig of a gnome! she thought. *The dirty little troll!*

Kelexel had been drinking from a flagon. He dipped it into the bowl, raised it dripping amber. "Good drink, delightful foods, comfortable clothing—all this and great enjoyment, amusement. Who could grow bored here?"

"Yes, indeed," Ruth muttered. "Who c'd grow bored?" Again, she drank deeply of the wine.

Kelexel took another sip from his flagon, adjusted his metabolism. Ruth's voice sounded so strange. He noted the manipulator's setting, wondered if he should apply a bit more pressure. Could it be the liquor? he asked himself.

"Did you enjoy yourself with the pantovive?" he asked.

The dirty, evil little troll! she thought. " 'S great fun," she sneered. "Why'ntch go play with it y'rself f'r awhile?"

"Lords of Preservation!" Kelexel muttered. He had just realized that the liquor was inhibiting Ruth's higher centers. Her head rolled crazily on her neck. She spilled part of her drink.

Kelexel reached over, took the glass from her, placed it gently on the table. She either was incapable or had never learned how to adjust her metabolism, he realized.

"Don'tcha like th' stories?" Ruth asked.

Kelexel began to remember, from Fraffin productions, the native problems involving various liquors. It was all true, then. *Real,* as Ruth would say.

" 'S a dirty world," she said. "Y' s'pose we're part of a story? They shootin' us with their damn cameras?"

What a hideous idea, Kelexel thought. But there was a strange sense of verity in her words. The dialogue carried some of the surface characteristics of a Fraffin story.

In this moment, Kelexel had to remind himself that creatures such as Ruth had lived long (by their standards) in dreams that Fraffin wove. Not exactly dreams, though, because Chem spectators, could enter the story world, too. In a sudden burst of insight, Kelexel realized he had entered the world of violence and emotion which Fraffin had created. Entering that world, he had been corrupted. To share the native delusions if only for a moment was to be enslaved by the need for more such corruption.

Kelexel wanted to tear himself away from this room, renounce his new pet, return only to his duty. But he knew he couldn't do that. Knowing this, he wondered what particular thing had trapped him. No answer came to his searching awareness.

He stared at Ruth.

These natives are a dangerous flame, he thought. *We don't own them! We're their slaves!*

Now, his suspicions were fully aroused. He stared around the room. What was it? What was wrong here?

He found nothing of this moment and this place upon which he could focus his educated suspicions. This of itself touched a deep chord of anger and fear in him. He felt that he was being played with, led about. Was Fraffin playing with him? The ship's people had suborned four previous Investigators of the Bureau. How? What plans had they for his own person? Surely they knew by now he was no ordinary visitor. But what could they possibly do?

Not violence, certainly.

Ruth began to cry, the sobs shaking her shoulders. "All alone," she muttered. "All alone."

Was it the native female? Kelexel wondered. Was she the bait in the trap?

There could be no certainty in a secret battle of this kind. You contended, one against the other, but every struggle occurred beneath a deceptively calm surface, hidden behind polite words and civilities and ritual behavior. The struggle went on and on within an intimate arena where no violence could be permitted.

How can they hope to win? Kelexel asked himself.

Even if they bested him, they must know there'd be other Kelexels. It would never end.

Never.

Never.

Awareness of an endless future broke like waves across the reef of his mind. On this path lay the Chem madness, Kelexel knew. He drew back from such thoughts.

Ruth got up, stood looking down at him unsteadily.

Savagely, Kelexel adjusted the manipulator. Ruth stiffened. The skin rippled on her cheeks and forearms. Her eyes glazed over. Abruptly, she turned, ran for the water basin in the corner. She leaned on it, retching.

Presently, she returned to her chair, moving as though pulled by strings. Distantly in her mind, a tiny kernel of awareness cried out: *"This is not you doing these things! These things are being done to you."*

Kelexel held up his flagon, said: "With such things as this your world fascinates and attracts us. Tell me, with what does your world repel?"

"It isn't a world," she said, her voice shaky. "It's a cage. This is your own private zoo."

"Ahhh, hmmm," Kelexel said. He sipped at his drink, but it had lost its savor. He put the flagon on the table. There were wet circles there where he had put the flagon before. He looked at them. The female was becoming resistant, obstinate. How could that be? Only the Chem and an occasional mutant were immune to such pressures. Even the Chem wouldn't be completely immune without Tiggywaugh's web and the special treatment they received at birth.

Again, he studied Ruth.

She returned his stare defiantly.

"Your lives are so short," Kelexel said. "Your past is so short—yet one gains the definite feeling of something ancient from you. How can that be?"

"Score one for our side," Ruth said. She could feel

her emotions being adjusted, soothed. It happened with an uncanny rapidity. Insane sobriety invaded her mind.

"Please stop changing me," she whispered.

And she wondered: *Was that the right thing to say then?* But she felt she had to disagree with the creature now, even risk making him angry. She had to oppose him—subtly, definitely. It was either that or lose her sanity in this wasteland of unreason. She could no longer remain passive, fencing in a mental world where the Chem could not come.

Stop changing her? Kelexel wondered.

There lay a kernel of opposition in that whispered cry and he recognized it. Thus the barbarian always spoke to the civilizer. Instantly alerted, he became at once the true cynic of the Federation, the loyal servant of the Primacy. The native female should not be *able* to oppose him.

"How do I change you?" he asked.

"I wish I knew," she said. "All I know is you think I'm stupid and don't realize what you're doing."

Has Fraffin trained this creature? Kelexel wondered. *Was she prepared for me?* He remembered his first interview with Fraffin, the sense of menace.

"What has Fraffin told you to do?" he demanded.

"Fraffin?" Her face showed blank puzzlement. What had the storyship's director to do with her?

"I won't betray you," Kelexel said.

She wet her lips with her tongue. Nothing the Chem did or said made any sense. The only thing she really understood was their power.

"If Fraffin's done anything illegal with you creatures I must know about it," Kelexel said. "I will not be denied. I *will* know about it."

She shook her head.

"As much as *can* be known of Fraffin, *that* I know," Kelexel said. "You were little more than the rawest sort of animals here when he came. Chem walked among you as gods then without the slightest concern."

"Illegal?" she said. "What do you mean illegal?"

"You've rudimentary laws among your kind," Kelexel sneered. "You know about legality and illegality."

"I've never even seen Fraffin," she said. "Except on the room screen."

"The letter of the law, eh? His minions, then—what have they told you to do?"

Again, she shook her head. There was a weapon here she could use; she sensed this, but couldn't quite understand enough to grasp it.

Kelexel whirled away from her, strode to the pantovive and back. He stopped ten paces from Ruth, glared up at her. "He bred you and shaped you and nudged you—*changed* you—into the finest story property in the universe. Some of the offers he's had—and turned down—would . . . well, you wouldn't understand."

"Turned down . . . why?" she asked.

"Ahh, that is the question."

"Why . . . why're we so valuable?"

He gestured, a handsweep that pointed from her feet to her hair. "You're gross and overgrown, but quite a bit similar to us. We can identify with you. There's entertainment in your strivings, a surcease from boredom."

"But you said—illegal?"

"When a race such as yours reaches a certain stage, there are . . . liberties we do not permit. We've had to exterminate certain races, severely punish a few Chem."

"But what . . . liberties?"

"Never mind." Kelexel turned his back on her. It seemed obvious she spoke from actual ignorance. Under such manipulator pressure she could hardly lie or dissemble.

Ruth stared at Kelexel's back. For long days now, a question had been creeping upward in her mind. The answer felt deeply important now. "How old are you?" she asked.

Slowly, Kelexel rotated on one heel, studied her. It took a moment to overcome the distaste aroused by such a gauche question, then: "How could that possibly bear on anything that concerns you?"

"It . . . I want to know."

"The actual duration—that's not important. But a hundred such worlds as yours, perhaps many more, could've come into being and dissolved to dust since my conception. Now, tell me why you want to know."

"I . . . just want to know." She tried to swallow in a dry throat. "How . . . how do you . . . preserve. . . ."

"Rejuvenation!" He shook his head. What a distasteful subject. The native female was truly barbaric.

"The woman Ynvic," Ruth said, sensing his emotional disturbance and enjoying it. "She's called the shipsurgeon. Does she supervise the. . . ."

"It's routine! Purely routine. We've elaborate protective mechanisms and devices that prevent anything but minor damage. A shipsurgeon takes care of the minor damage. Very rare, that. We can take care of our own regenerative and rejuvenating treatments. Now, you will tell me why you ask."

"Could I . . . we. . . ."

"Oh, ho!" Kelexel threw his head back in a bark of laughter. Then: "You must be a Chem and conditioned for the process from birth or it cannot be done."

"But . . . you're like us. You . . . breed."

"Not with you, my dear pet. We're pleasurably similar, that I admit. But with you it's dalliance, insulation from boredom, no more. We Chem cannot breed with any other. . . ." He broke off, stared at her, remembering a conversation with Ynvic. They'd been discussing the native violence, wars.

"It's a built-in valving system to keep down the immunes," Ynvic had said.

"The conflicts?"

"Of course. A person immune to our manipulations tends to become generally dissatisfied, frustrated. Such creatures welcome violence and disregard personal safety. The attrition rate among them is very high."

Remembering Ynvic's words, Kelexel wondered: *Is it possible? No! It couldn't be! Gene samples from these natives were on record long ago. I've seen them myself. But what if. . . . No! There's no way. But it would be so simple: falsify the gene sample. Shipsurgeon Ynvic! But if she did, why?* Kelexel shook his head. The whole idea was preposterous. *Even Fraffin wouldn't dare breed a planet full of half-Chem. The immune ratio would give him away before. . . . But there's always the "valving system."*

"I will see Fraffin now," Kelexel muttered.

And he remembered: *"Ynvic was referring to native immunes, but she said person."*

15

FRAFFIN SAT WAITING BEHIND HIS DESK AS KELEXEL
entered the director's salon. The room's silver light had
been tuned to a high pitch, almost glaring. The surface
of the desk glittered. Fraffin wore native dress, a black
suit with white linen tie. Golden buttons at the cuffs reflected shards of brilliance into Kelexel's eyes.

Behind a mask of brooding superiority, Fraffin felt
himself poised for a pouncing elation. This poor fool of
an Investigator! The man had been aimed at his
present moment like an arrow. It only remained for
him to find the sort of target in which he'd been
embedded.

And I aimed him! Fraffin thought. *I put him here as
surely as I put any native into its predicament.*

"You asked to see me?" Fraffin asked. He remained
seated, emphasizing his displeasure with the visitor.

Kelexel noted the gesture, ignored it. Fraffin's pos-
ture was almost boorish. Perhaps it reflected confidence
and that would bear watching. But the Primacy did not
send complete fools to do its investigating and the
Director must discover this soon.

"I wish to discuss my pet with you," Kelexel said,
seating himself across from Fraffin without invitation.
The desk was an enormous empty expanse separat-
ing them. A faint glistening reflection of Fraffin could
be seen in its surface.

"There's something wrong with your pet?" Fraffin
asked. He smiled to himself, thinking of the latest report on Kelexel's antics with the native female. The
Investigator was suspicious now; no doubt of that. But
too late—far too late.

"Perhaps there's nothing wrong with my pet,"

Kelexel said. "Certainly she delights me. But it has occurred to me that I know so little really about the natives, her sources, so to speak."

"And you came to *me* to fill out this information?"

"I felt certain you'd see me," Kelexel said. He waited, wondering if that barb would sink home. Surely, it was time they brought the battle more into the open.

Fraffin sat back, eyelids drooping, silver-blue shadows in the sockets. He nodded to himself. Ahh, it was going to be good sport playing out this fool's downfall. Fraffin savored the anticipatory moment, the instant of revelation.

Kelexel put his hands on the arms of his chair, felt clean edges of construction, a gentle warmth. A distant musky aroma permeated the room, an exotic tantalizing thing full of alien strangeness . . . a floral essence perhaps.

"But you enjoy your pet?" Fraffin asked.

"A delight," Kelexel said. "Better even than the Subi. I wonder that you don't export them. Why is that?"

"So you've had a Subi," Fraffin said, parrying the question.

"I still wonder that you don't export these females," Kelexel said. "I find it very odd."

Oh, you find it odd, Fraffin thought. He experienced an abrupt sour feeling about Kelexel. The man was so obviously besotten with the native female—his first experience with them.

"There are many collectors who'd leap at the chance to have one of these natives," Kelexel said, probing. "Of all the delights you've gathered here. . . ."

"And you think I've nothing better to do than collect my natives for the delight of my fellows," Fraffin said. His voice sounded snappish and he wondered at the emotion in it. *Am I jealous of Kelexel?* he asked himself.

"Then what is your task here if not to make profit?" Kelexel asked. He could feel himself growing angry with Fraffin. Certainly, the Director knew he faced an

Investigator. But none of Fraffin's actions betrayed fear.

"I'm a collector of gossip," Fraffin said. "That I create some of this gossip myself, that is of no moment."

Gossip? Kelexel wondered.

And Fraffin thought: *A collector of ancient gossip—yes.*

He knew then that he was jealous of Kelexel, envious of the man's first encounter with a native female. Fraffin remembered the old days when the Chem had moved more openly on this world, creating the machinery of long maturation which they could exploit—devising leprous diplomats full of pride's blind ignorance, nurturing death wishes to ride each back like a demon. Ahhh, those had been the days.

Fraffin felt himself stretched for a moment on the rack of his own vision, remembering days when he'd lived among the natives—manipulating, maneuvering, eavesdropping, learning, listening to sniggering Roman boys talks of things their elders had forgotten even to whisper. In his mind, Fraffin saw his own villa with sunglow on a brick walk, grass, a tree, a planting of petulant forsythia. That's what *she'd* called them—"petulant forsythia." How clearly he could see in his mind the young pear tree beside the walk.

"They die so easily," he whispered.

Kelexel put a finger to his cheek, said: "I think you're just a touch morbid—all this emphasis on violence and death."

It wasn't in the plan, but Fraffin couldn't help himself. He glared at Kelexel, said: "You think you hate such things, eh? No, you don't! You say you're attracted by such things as this pretty native of yours. I hear you fancy the native clothing." He touched a sleeve of his jacket, a curious caressing gesture. "How little you know yourself, Kelexel."

Kelexel's face went dark with anger. This was too much! Fraffin exceeded all bounds of propriety!

"We Chem have locked the door on death and violence," he muttered. "Viewing it as a dalliance, no more."

"'Morbid, you say?" Fraffin asked. "We've locked the door on death? No longer for us, is it?" He chuckled. "Yet, there it stands, our eternal temptation. What do I do here that attracts you so—attracts you so much that in the very voice of admission you inquire about that which repels? I'll tell you what I do here: I play with temptations that my fellow Chem may watch."

Fraffin's hands moved as he talked—chopping, cutting gestures that exposed the ever-young flesh, active, vibrant—small hairs curling on the back of the fingers, nails blunt, flat.

Kelexel stared at the man, caught in the spell of Fraffin's words. *Death—temptation? Surely not!* Yet, there was a cold certainty in the idea.

Watching Fraffin's hands, Kelexel thought: *The hand must not overthrow the mind.*

"You laugh," Kelexel said. "You think me amusing."

"Not *just* you," Fraffin said. "All is amusement— the poor creatures of my caged world and every last blessed one of us who cannot hear the warnings of our own eternal lives. All warnings have one exception, eh? Yourself! That's what I see and that's what amuses me. You laugh at *them* in my productions, but you don't know why you laugh. Ahh, Kelexel, here's where we hide the awareness of our own mortality."

Kelexel spoke in shocked outrage: "We're *not* mortal!"

"Kelexel, Kelexel—we're mortal. Any of us can end it, cease the rejuvenation, and that's mortal. That's mortal."

Kelexel sat silently staring. The Director was insane!

For Fraffin, the everlasting awareness which his own words had aroused foamed across his mind and, receding, exposed his rage.

I'm angry and remorseful, he thought. *I've accepted a morality no other Chem would entertain for a moment. I'm sorry for Kelexel and for all the creatures I've moved and removed without their knowing. They sprout fifty heads within me for every one I cut off. Gossip? A Collector of gossip? I'm a person of sensi-*

tive ears who can still hear a knife scraping toast in a villa that no longer exists.

He remembered the woman then—the dark, exotic chatelaine of his Roman home. She'd been no taller than himself, stunted by native standards, but lovely in his sight—the best of them all. She'd borne him eight mortal children, their mixed blood concealed in the genetic melt. She'd grown old and dull of face—and he remembered that too. Remembering her blunted look, he saw the black throng, the mixed-up disasters of their mingled genes. She'd given him something no other could: a share in mortality that he could accept for his own.

What the Primacy wouldn't give to know about that little interlude, he thought.

"You talk like a madman," Kelexel whispered.

We contend openly now, eh? Fraffin thought. *Perhaps I move too slowly with this dolt. Perhaps I should tell him now how he's caught in our trap.* But Fraffin felt himself swept up in the flow of his own anger. He couldn't help himself.

"A madman?" he asked, his voice sneering. "You say we're immortal, we Chem. How're we immortal? We rejuvenate and rejuvenate. We achieve a balance point, frozen short of final destruction. At what stage in our development, Chem Kelexel, are we frozen?"

"Stage?" Kelexel stared at him. Fraffin's words were firebrands.

"Yes, stage! Are we frozen in maturity? I think, not. To mature one must flower. We don't flower, Kelexel."

"I don't. . . ."

"We don't produce something of beauty and loveliness, something which is the essence of ourselves! We don't flower."

"I've had offspring!"

Fraffin couldn't contain his laughter. When it subsided, he faced a now openly angry Kelexel, said: "The unflowering seed, the perpetual immaturity producing the perpetual immaturity—and you brag about it! How mean and empty and frightened you are, Kelexel."

"What've I to fear?" Kelexel demanded. "Death can't touch me. *You* can't touch me!"

"Except from within," Fraffin said. "Death can't touch a Chem except from within. We're sovereign individuals, immortal citadels of selfdom that no force can storm . . . except from within. In each of us there's that seed out of our past, the seed which whispers: 'Remember? Remember when *we* could die?' "

Kelexel pushed himself upright, stood glaring down at Fraffin. "You're insane!"

"Sit down, *visitor*," Fraffin said. And he wondered at himself. *Why do I goad him? To justify myself in what I must do? If that's so, then I should give him something he can use against me. I should make this a more equal contest.*

Kelexel sank back into his seat. He reminded himself that the Chem were mostly immune to the more bizarre forms of madness, but one never knew what stresses might be imposed by outpost living, by contact with an alien race. The boredom psychosis threatened all of them—perhaps Fraffin had succumbed to something in that syndrome.

"Let us see if you have a conscience," Fraffin said.

It was such an unexpected statement that Kelexel could only goggle at him. There came a sense of furtive emptying within himself, though, and Kelexel recognized peril in Fraffin's words.

"What harm could there be in that?" Fraffin asked. He turned. Earlier one of the crew had brought a vase of roses and put them on the cabinet behind his desk. Fraffin looked at the roses. They were full blown, dripping blood-colored petals like the garlands on Diana's altar. *There's no more joking in Sumeria,* he thought. *No more do we jest, inserting foolishness into Minerva's wisdom.*

"What are you talking about?" Kelexel asked.

For answer, Fraffin moved a control stud beneath his desk. His pantovive reproducer whirred into action, slid across the room like a giant beast and positioned itself at Fraffin's right where they would share the view of its focusing stage.

Kelexel stared at it, suddenly dry-mouthed. The frivolous entertainment machine was a sudden monster that he feared was capable of striking him unaware.

"It was thoughtful of you to provide one of these for your pet," Fraffin said. "Shall we see what she's watching?"

"How can that concern us?" Kelexel demanded. He heard anger and uncertainty in his own voice, knew Fraffin was aware of this reaction.

"Let us see," Fraffin said. He swung the bank of control studs within easy reach, moved them lovingly. The stage became a native room up there on the planet surface—a long, narrow room with beige plaster walls, a washed brown ceiling. The view looked directly along a burn-scarred plank table that jutted from a steam radiator which hissed beneath the red and white curtains of a barred window.

Two men sat facing each other across the table.

"Ahh," Fraffin said. "On the left we have your pet's father, and on the right we have the man she'd have mated with had we not stepped in and given her to you."

"Stupid, useless natives," Kelexel sneered.

"But she's watching them right now," Fraffin said. "This is what's going into her pantovive . . . which you so kindly provided."

"She's quite happy here; I'm sure of it," Kelexel said.

"Then why don't you release her from the manipulator?" Fraffin asked.

"When she's fully conditioned," Kelexel said. "She'll be more than content to serve a Chem when she understands what we can provide her."

"Of course," Fraffin said. He studied Andy Thurlow's profile. The lips moved, but Fraffin kept the sound bar turned off. "That's why she watches this scene from my current production."

"What's so important about this scene?" Kelexel demanded. "Perhaps she's caught by your artistry."

"Indeed," Fraffin said.

Kelexel studied the native on the left. His pet's father? He noted how the native's eyelids drooped. This was a heavy-featured creature with an air of secretiveness about it. The native might almost have been a gross Chem. How could that thing have fathered the slender grace of his pet?

"The one she'd have mated with is a native witch doctor," Fraffin said.

"Witch doctor?"

"They prefer to be called psychologists. Shall we listen to them?"

"As you said: What harm could there be in that?"

Fraffin moved the sound bar. "Yes, indeed."

"Perhaps it'll be amusing," Kelexel said, but there was no amusement in his voice. Why did his pet watch these creatures out of her past? This could only torment her.

"Shhh," Fraffin said.

"What?"

"Listen!"

Thurlow bent to arrange a stack of papers on the table. The sound was a faint hissing. There came the smell of dusty air, stale and full of strange essences, as the sensi-mesh web encompassed Kelexel and Fraffin.

Joe Murphey's guttural voice rumbled from the stage: "I'm surprised to see you, Andy. Heard you had some sort of attack."

"It must've been the one-day flu," Thurlow said. "Everybody's been having it."

(Fraffin chuckled.)

"Any word from Ruthy?" Murphey asked.

"No."

"You've lost her again, that's what. Thought I told you to take care of her. But maybe women's all alike."

Thurlow adjusted his glasses, looked up and straight into the eyes of the watching Chem.

Kelexel gasped.

"What do you make of that?" Fraffin whispered.

"An immune!" Kelexel hissed. And he thought: *I have Fraffin now! Allowing an immune to watch his shooting crew!* He asked: "Is the creature still alive?"

"We recently gave him a little taste of our power," Fraffin said, "but I find him too amusing to destroy."

Murphey cleared his throat and Kelexel sat back, watching, listening. *Destroy yourself, then, Fraffin,* he thought.

"You wouldn't get sick if you were in here," Murphey said. "I've gained weight on this jailhouse diet. What surprises me is how well I've adjusted to the routine here."

Thurlow returned his attention to the papers in front of him.

Kelexel felt himself caught by the creatures' actions, sensed himself sinking out of sight into these other beings, becoming a bundle of watchful senses. One irritant remained to gnaw at him, though: *Why does she watch these creatures from her past?*

"Things are going along all right, eh?" Thurlow asked. He stacked inkblot cards in front of Murphey.

"Well it does drag," Murphey said. "Things're slow here." He tried not to look at the cards.

"But you think jail agrees with you?"

Fraffin manipulated the pantovive controls. Point of view moved closer to the natives. The two figures became enlarged profiles. (Kelexel experienced the eerie sensation that his own flesh had been moved, pushed forward to a new vantage.)

"We're going to run these cards a little differently this time," Thurlow said. "You've been having these tests so frequently, I want to change the pace."

An abrupt crouching look came over Murphey's hunched shoulders, but his voice emerged open and bland: "Anything you say, Doc."

"I'll sit here facing you," Thurlow said. "That's a bit unorthodox, but this situation's full of irregularities."

"You mean you knowing me and all?"

"Yes." Thurlow placed a stopwatch beside him on the table. "And I've changed the usual order of the cards."

The stopwatch exerted a sudden attraction for Murphey. He stared at it. A faint tremor moved up his thick forearms. With a visible effort, he arranged his features into a look of eager brightness, a willingness to cooperate.

"You sat behind me last time," he said. "So did Doctor Whelye."

"I know," Thurlow said. He busied himself checking the order of the cards.

Kelexel jumped as Fraffin touched his arm, looked up to see the director leaning across the desk. "This Thurlow's good," Fraffin whispered. "Watch him carefully. Notice how he changes the test. There's a learning element involved in having the same test several times in a short period. It's like being put in jeopardy enough times until you learn how to avoid the danger."

Kelexel heard the double meaning in Fraffin's words, watched as the Director sank back, smiling. A sense of unease came over Kelexel then. He returned his attention to the pantovive stage. What was the importance of this scene, this confession of guilt? A conscience? He studied Thurlow, wondering if Ruth were released would she go back to that creature. How could she after experiencing a Chem?

A pang of jealousy shot through Kelexel. He sat back, scowled.

Thurlow now gave evidence of being ready to start his test. He exposed the first card, started his stopwatch, kept a hand on it.

Murphey stared at the first card, pursed his lips. Presently, he said: "Been a car accident. Two people killed. That's their bodies beside the road. Lotsa accidents nowadays. People just don't know how to handle fast cars."

"Are you isolating part of the pattern or does the whole card give you that picture?" Thurlow asked.

Murphey blinked. "Just this little part here." He turned the card face down, lifted the second one. "This is a will or a deed like to property, but somebody's let it fall in the water and the writing's all smeared. That's how you can't read it."

"A will? Any idea whose?"

Murphey gestured with the card. "You know, when grandpaw died they never found the will. He had one. We all knew he had one, but Uncle Amos wound up with most of Gramp's stuff. That's how I learned to be careful with my papers. You've gotta be careful with important papers."

"Was your father cautious like that?"

"Paw? Hell, no!"

Thurlow appeared caught by something in Murphey's tone. He said: "You and your father ever fight?"

"Jawed some, that's all."

"You mean argued."

"Yeah. He always wanted me to stay with the mules and wagon."

Thurlow sat waiting, watchful, studying.

Murphey assumed a death's head grin. "That's an old saying we had in the family." Abruptly, he put down the card in his hand, took up the third one. He cocked his head to one side. "Hide of a muskrat stretched out to dry. They brought eleven cents apiece when I was a boy."

Thurlow said: "Try for another association. See if you can find something else in the card."

Murphey flicked a glance at Thurlow, back to the card. An appearance of spring-wound tension came over him. The silence dragged out.

Watching the scene, Kelexel had the sensation that Thurlow was reaching through Murphey to the pantovive's audience. He felt that he himself was being examined by the witch doctor. Logically, Kelexel knew this scene already lay in the past, that it was a captured record. There was an immediacy about it, though, a sensation of moving freely in time.

Again Murphey looked at Thurlow. "It might be a dead bat," he said. "Somebody might've shot it."

"Oh? Why would anyone do that?"

"Because they're dirty!" Murphey put the card on the table, pushed it away from him. He looked concerned. Slowly, he reached for the next card, exposed it as though fearful of what he might find.

Thurlow checked the watch, returned his attention to Murphey.

Murphey studied the card in his hand. Several times he appeared about to speak. Each time he hesitated, remained silent. Presently, he said: "Fourth of July rockets, the fire kind that go off in the air. Dangerous damn' things."

"The explosive kind?" Thurlow asked.

Murphey peered at the card. "Yeah, the kind that

explode and shoot out stars. Those stars can start fires."

"Have you ever seen one start a fire?"

"I've heard about it."

"Where?"

"Lotsa places! Every year they warn people about those damn' things. Don't you read the papers?"

Thurlow made a note on the pad in front of him.

Murphey glowered at him a moment, went on to the next card. "This one's a drawing of where they've poisoned an ant hill and cut the hill in half to map out how the holes were dug."

Thurlow leaned back, his attention concentrated on Murphey's face. "Why would someone make such a map?"

"To see how the ants work it out. I fell on an ant hill when I was a kid. They bit like fire. Maw put soda on me. Paw poured coal oil on the hill and set a match to it. Man, did they scatter! Paw jumping all around, smashing 'em."

With a reluctant motion, Murphey put down the card, took up the next one. He glared at Thurlow's hand making notes, turned his attention to the card. A charged silence settled over him.

Staring at the card in Murphey's hand, Kelexel saw Chem flitters against a sunset sky, a fleet of them going from nowhere to nowhere. He experienced a sudden fearful wondering at what Thurlow might say to this.

Murphey extended the card at arm's length, squinted his eyes. "Over on the left there it could be that mountain in Switzerland where people're always falling off and getting killed."

"The Matterhorn?"

"Yeah."

"Does the rest of the card suggest anything to you?"

Murphey tossed the card aside. "Nothing."

Thurlow made a notation on the pad, looked up at Murphey who was studying the next card.

"All the times I've seen this card," Murphey said. "I never noticed this place up at the top." He pointed. "Right up here. It's a shipwreck with lifeboats sticking up out of the water. These little dots are the drowned people."

Thurlow swallowed. He appeared to be debating a comment. With an abrupt leaning foward, he asked: "Were there any survivors?"

A look of sad reluctance came over Murphey's face. "No," he sighed. "This was a bad one. You know, my Uncle Al died the year the Titanic sank."

"Was he on the Titanic?"

"No. That's just how I fix the date. Helps you remember. Like when that Zeppelin burned, that was the year I moved my company into the new building."

Murphey went to the next card, smiled. "Here's an easy one. It's a mushroom cloud from an atomic bomb."

Thurlow wet his lips with his tongue, then: "The whole card?"

"No, just this white place here at the side." He pointed. "It's . . . like a photograph of the explosion."

Murphey's blocky hand shuffled to the next card. He held it close, squinting down at it. An air of brooding silence settled over the room.

Kelexel glanced at Fraffin, found the director studying him.

"What's the purpose of all this?" Kelexel whispered.

"You're whispering," Fraffin said. "Don't you want Thurlow to hear you?"

"What?"

"These native witch doctors have strange powers," Fraffin said. "They're very penetrating at times."

"It's a lot of nonsense," Kelexel said. "Mumbo jumbo. The test doesn't mean a thing. The native's answers are perfectly logical. I might've said comparable things myself."

"Indeed?" Fraffin said.

Kelexel remained silent, returned his attention to the pantovive stage. Murphey was peering warily at Thurlow.

"Part through the middle might be a forest fire," Murphey said. He watched Thurlow's mouth.

"Have you ever seen a forest fire?"

"Where one'd been. Stank to heaven with dead cows. Burned out a ranch up on the Siuslaw."

Thurlow wrote on the pad.

Murphey glared at him, swallowed, turned to the final card. As he looked at it, he drew in a sharp, hard breath as though he'd been hit in the stomach.

Thurlow looked up quickly, studied him.

A look of confusion passed over Murphey's face. He squirmed in his chair, then: "Is this one of the regular cards?"

"Yes."

"I don't remember it."

"Oh. Do you remember all the other cards?"

"Kind of."

"What about this card?"

"I think you've rung in a new one."

"No. It's one of the regular Rorschach cards."

Murphey turned a hard stare on the psychologist, said: "I had a right to kill her, Doc. Let's remember that. I had a right. A husband has to protect his home."

Thurlow sat quietly waiting.

Murphey jerked his attention back to the card. "A junkyard," he blurted. "It reminds me of a junkyard."

Still, Thurlow remained silent.

"Wrecked cars, old boilers, things like that," Murphey said. He tossed the card aside, sat back with a look of cautious waiting.

Thurlow took a deep breath, collected the cards and data sheets, slipped them into a briefcase which he lifted from the floor beside his chair. Slowly, he turned, stared directly into the pantovive.

Kelexel had the disquieting sensation that Thurlow was staring him in the eyes.

"Tell me, Joe," Thurlow said, "what do you see there?" He pointed at the pantovive's watchers.

"Huh? Where?"

"There." Thurlow continued to point.

Murphey now stared out of the pantovive at the audience. "Some dust or smoke," he said. "They don't keep this place too clean."

"But what do you see in the dust or smoke?" Thurlow persisted. He lowered his hand.

Murphey squinted, tipped his head to one side, "Ohh, maybe it's kinda like a lot of little faces . . . babies' faces, like cherubs or . . . no, like those imps they put in pictures of hell."

Thurlow turned back to the prisoner. "Imps of hell," he murmured. "How very appropriate."

At the pantovive, Fraffin slapped the cutoff. The scene faded from the stage.

Kelexel blinked, turned, was surprised to find Fraffin chuckling.

"Imps of hell," Fraffin said. "Oh, that's lovely. That is purely lovely."

"You're deliberately allowing an immune to watch us and record our actions," Kelexel said. "I see nothing lovely about that!"

"What did you think of Murphey?" Fraffin asked.

"He looked as sane as I am."

A spasm of laughter overcame Fraffin. He shook his head, rubbed his eyes, then: "Murphey's my own creation, Kelexel. My own creation. I've shaped him most carefully and certainly from his infancy. Isn't he delightful. Imps of hell!"

"Is he an immune, too?"

"Lords of Preservation, no!"

Kelexel studied the Director. Surely Fraffin had penetrated the disguise by now. Why would he betray himself, flaunt an immune before an Investigator from the Primacy? Was it the witch doctor? Had these natives some mysterious power which Fraffin could use?

"I don't understand your motives, Fraffin," Kelexel said.

"That's obvious," Fraffin said. "What about Thurlow. Does it give you no pangs of guilt to watch the creature you've robbed of a mate?"

"The . . . witch doctor? The immune? He must be disposed of. How can I rob him of anything? It's a Chem's right to take whatever he desires from the lower orders."

"But . . . Thurlow's almost human, don't you think?"

"Nonsense!"

"No, no, Kelexel. He has a great native capability.

He's superb. Couldn't you see how he was drawing Murphey out, exposing the flesh of insanity?"

"How can you say the native's insane?"

"He is, Kelexel. I made him that way."

"I . . . don't believe you."

"Patience and courtesy," Fraffin said. "What would you say if I told you I could show you more of Thurlow without your seeing him at all?"

Kelexel sat up straight. He felt wary, as though all his previous fears had come back amplified. Bits of the scene Fraffin had just shown reeled through his mind, clinging and wisping away, their meanings changed and distorted. Insane? And what of Ruth, his pet? She had watched that scene, perhaps was still watching more of it. Why would she wish to see such a . . . painful thing. It must be painful for her. It must be. For the first time in his memory, Kelexel felt himself drawn to share another being's emotions. He tried to shake it off. She was a native, one of the lower orders. He looked up to find Fraffin staring at him. It was as though they had exchanged places with the two natives they'd just watched. Fraffin had assumed the role of Thurlow and he, Kelexel, was Murphey.

What powers has he gained from these natives? Kelexel asked himself. *Can he see into me, divine my thoughts? But I'm not insane . . . or violent.*

"What paradox is this you propose?" Kelexel demanded. And he was proud that his voice remained level, calm and questing.

Gently, gently, Fraffin thought. *He's well hooked, but he mustn't struggle with me too much—not yet.*

"An amusing thing," Fraffin said. "Observe." He gestured at the pantovive's stage, manipulated the controls.

Kelexel turned reluctantly, stared at the projected scene—the same drab room, the same barred window with its red and white curtains, the hissing radiator, Murphey seated in the same position at the scarred table. It was a tableau, identical with the scene they'd just watched except that another native sat behind Murphey, his back to the observers, a clipboard and papers on his knees.

Like Murphey, this new figure conveyed an impression of excessive bulk. The visible curve of cheek when he turned his head showed choleric. The back of his neck carried a sanitary, barber-scraped appearance.

A scattered stack of the inkblot cards lay on the table before Murphey. He was tapping a finger on the back of one of them.

As Kelexel studied the scene, he observed a subtle difference in Murphey. There was a suggestion of greater calm. He was more relaxed, more sure of himself.

Fraffin cleared his throat, said: "The native writing on that pad is another witch doctor, Whelye, an associate of Thurlow's. He has just finished administering the same test to Murphey. Observe him carefully."

"Why?" Kelexel asked. This repetition of native rites was beginning to bore him.

"Just observe," Fraffin said.

Abruptly, Murphey picked up the card he'd been tapping, looked at it, discarded it.

Whelye turned, raised his head to expose a round face, two buttons of blue eyes, a steep shelf of nose and thin mouth. Satisfaction poured from him as though it were a light he shone on everything within range of his senses. In the satisfaction there lay a stalking craftiness.

"That card," he said, his voice petulant. "Why'd you look at that card again?"

"I . . . ah, just wanted another look," Murphey said. He lowered his head.

"Do you see something new in it?"

"What I always see in it—an animal skin."

Whelye stared at the back of Murphey's head with a look of glee. "An animal skin, the kind you trapped when you were a boy."

"I made a lot of money off those skins. Always had an eye for money."

Whelye's head bobbed up and down, a curious wracking motion that rippled a fold of flesh against his collar. "Would you like a second look at any of the other cards?"

Murphey wet his lips with his tongue. "Guess not."

"Interesting," Whelye murmured.

Murphey turned slightly, spoke without looking at the psychiatrist. "Doc, maybe you'd tell me something."

"What?"

"I had this test from another of you headshrinkers, you know—from Thurlow. What's it show?"

Something fierce and pouncing arose in Whelye's face. "Didn't Thurlow tell you?"

"No. I figured you're more of a right guy, that you'd level with me."

Whelye looked down at the papers in his lap, moved his pencil absently. He began filling in the "o's" of a printed line. "Thurlow has no medical degree."

"Yeah, but what's the test show about me?"

Whelye completed his pencil work on the line of print, sat back and examined it. "It takes a little time to evaluate the data," he said, "but I'd hazard a guess you're as normal as the next fellow."

"Does that mean I'm sane?" Murphey asked. He stared at the table, breath held, waiting.

"As sane as I am," Whelye said.

A deep sigh escaped Murphey. He smiled, looked sidelong at the inkblot cards. "Thanks, Doc."

The scene faded abruptly.

Kelexel shook his head, looked across the desk to see Fraffin's hand on the pantovive's cutoff controls. The Director was grinning at him.

"See," Fraffin said. "Someone else who thinks Murphey's sane, someone who agrees with you."

"You said you were going to show me Thurlow."

"But I did!"

"I don't understand."

"Didn't you see the compulsive way this witch doctor filled in those letters on his paper? Did you see Thurlow doing anything like that?"

"No, but. . . ."

"And didn't you notice how much this witch doctor enjoyed Murphey's fear?"

"But fear *can* be amusing at times."

"And pain, and violence?" Fraffin asked.

"Certainly, if they're handled correctly."

Fraffin continued to stare at him, smiling.

I enjoy their fear, too, Kelexel thought. *Is that what this insane director's suggesting? Is he trying to compare me to these . . . creatures? Any Chem enjoys such things!*

"Some of these natives have conceived the strange idea," Fraffin said, "that anything which degrades life—degrades *any* life—is a sickness."

"But that depends entirely on what form of life's degraded," Kelexel objected. "Surely, even these natives of yours wouldn't hesitate to degrade a . . . a . . . a worm!"

Fraffin merely stared at him.

"Well?" Kelexel demanded.

Still Fraffin stared.

Kelexel felt his rage rising. He glared at Fraffin.

"It's merely an idea," Fraffin said, "something to toy with. Ideas are our toys, too, aren't they?"

"An insane idea," Kelexel growled.

He reminded himself then that he was here to remove the menace of this storyship's mad director. And the man had exposed his crime! It would bring severe censure and relocation at the very least. And if this were widespread—ah, then! Kelexel sat studying Fraffin, savoring the coming moment of denunciation, the righteous anger, the threat of eternal ostracism from his own kind. Let Fraffin go into the outer blackness of eternal boredom! Let this madman discover what *Forever* really meant!

The thought lay there a moment in Kelexel's mind. He had never approached it from quite this point of view before. Forever. *What does it really mean?* he asked himself.

He tried to imagine himself isolated, thrown onto his own resources for time-without-end. His mind recoiled from the thought, and he felt a twinge of pity for what might happen to Fraffin.

"Now," Fraffin said. "Now is the moment."

Can he be goading me to denounce him? Kelexel wondered. *It isn't possible!*

"It's my pleasant task to tell you," Fraffin said, "that you're going to have another offspring."

Kelexel sat staring, stupefied by the words. He tried

to speak, couldn't. Presently, he found his voice, rasped: "But how can you. . . ."

"Oh, not in the legally approved manner," Fraffin said, "There'll be no delicate little operation, no optimum selection of ovarian donor from the banks in the Primacy's crèche. Nothing that simple."

"What do you. . . ."

"Your native pet," Fraffin said. "You've impregnated her. She's going to bear your child in the . . . ancient way, as we once did before the orderly organization of the Primacy."

"That . . . that's impossible," Kelexel whispered.

"Not at all," Fraffin said. "You see, what we have here is a planet full of wild Chem."

Kelexel sat silently absorbing the evil beauty of Fraffin's revelation, seeing the breath behind the words, seeing things here as he was meant to see them. The crime was so simple. So simple! Once he overcame the mental block that occluded thinking about such matters, the whole structure fell into place. It was a crime fitting Fraffin's stature, a crime such as no other Chem had ever conceived. A perverse admiration for Fraffin seeped through Kelexel.

"You are thinking," Fraffin said, "that you have but to denounce me and the Primacy will set matters right. Attend the consequences. The creatures of this planet will be sterilized so as not to contaminate the Chem bloodlines. The planet will be shut down until we can put it to some *proper* use. Your new offspring, a half-breed, will go with the rest."

Abruptly, Kelexel sensed forgotten instincts begin to war in him. The threat in Fraffin's words opened a hoard of things Kelexel had thought locked away. He'd never suspected the potency or danger of these forces he'd supposed were chained—forever. Odd thoughts buzzed in his mind like caged birds. Something free and wild rose in him and he thought:

Imagine having an unlimited number of offspring!

Then: *So this is what happened to the other Investigators!*

In this instant, Kelexel knew he had lost.

"Will you let them destroy your offspring?" Fraffin asked.

The question was redundant. Kelexel had already posed it and answered it. No Chem would hazard his own offspring—so rare and precious a thing, that lonely link with the lost past. He sighed.

In the sigh, Fraffin saw victory and smiled.

Kelexel's thoughts turned inward. The Primacy had lost another round with Fraffin. The precise and formal way he had participated in that loss grew clearer to Kelexel by the minute. There was the blind (was it really blind?) way he'd walked into the trap. He'd been as easy for Fraffin to manipulate as any of the wild creatures on this wonderful world.

The realization that he must accept defeat, that he had no choice, brought an odd feeling of happiness to Kelexel. It wasn't joy, but a backward sorrow as poignant and profound as grief.

I will have an unlimited supply of female pets, he thought. *And they will give me offspring.*

A cloud passed across his mind then and he spoke to Fraffin as a fellow conspirator: "What if the Primacy sends a *female* Investigator?"

"Make our task easier," Fraffin said. "Chem females, deprived of the ability to breed, but *not* deprived of the instinct, find great joy here. They dabble in the pleasures of the flesh, of course. Native males have a wonderful lack of inhibitions. But the magnetic attraction for our females is a very simple thing. One exposure and they're addicted to watching at the births! They get some vicarious pleasure out of it that I don't understand, but Ynvic assures me it's profound."

Kelexel nodded. It must be true. The females in this conspiracy must be held by some strong tie. But Kelexel was still the Investigator in his training. He noted the way Fraffin's mouth moved, the creasing of lines at the eyes: little betrayals. There was an element here that Fraffin was refusing to recognize. The battle would be lost some day. Forever was too long for the Primacy to lose every exchange. Suspicions would mount to certainty and then *any* means would be employed to unveil this secret.

Seeing this, Kelexel felt a pang of grief. It was as though the inevitable already had happened. Here was an outpost of the Chem mortality and it, too, would go—in time. Here was a part of all Chem that rebelled against *Forever*. Here was the proof that somewhere in every Chem, the fact of immortality hadn't been accepted. But the evidence would be erased.

"We'll find you a planet of your own," Fraffin said.

The instant he'd spoken, Fraffin wondered if he'd been too precipitate. Kelexel might need time to digest things. He'd appeared to stiffen there, but now he was rising, the polite Chem taking his leave, accepting defeat—no doubt going to be rejuvenated. He'd see the need for that at once, of course.

16

KELEXEL LAY FACE UP ON THE BED, HIS HANDS BEHIND his head, watching Ruth pace the floor. Back and forth, back and forth she went, her green robe hissing against her legs. She did this almost every time he came here now—unless he set the manipulator at a disgustingly high pressure.

His eyes moved to follow the pacing. Her robe was belted at the waist with emeralds chained in silver that glittered under the room's yellow light. Her body gave definite visible hints of her pregnancy—a mounding of the abdomen, a rich glow to her skin. She knew her condition, of course, but aside from one outburst of hysterics (which the manipulator controlled quickly) she made no mention of it.

Only ten rest periods had passed since his interview with Fraffin, yet Kelexel felt the past which had terminated in the director's salon had receded into dimness. The "amusing little story" centered on Ruth's parent had been recorded and terminated. (Kelexel found it less amusing every time he viewed it.) All that remained was to find a suitable outpost planet for his own uses.

Back and forth Ruth paced. She'd be at the pantovive in a moment, he knew. She hadn't used it yet in his presence, but he could see her glancing at it. He could sense the machine drawing her into its orbit.

Kelexel glanced up at the manipulator controlling her emotions. The strength of its setting frightened him. She'd be immune to it one day; no doubt of that. The manipulator was a great metal insect spread over the ceiling.

Kelexel sighed.

Now that he knew Ruth was a wild Chem, her ancestry heavily infused with storyship bloodlines, he found his feelings about her disturbed. She had become more than a creature, almost a *person*.

Was it right to manipulate a person? Wrong? Right? Conscience? The attitudes of this world's exotics infused strange doubts into him. Ruth wasn't full Chem—never could be. She hadn't been taken in infancy, transformed and stunted by immortality. She was marked down at no position in Tiggywaugh's web.

What would the Primacy do when they found out? Was Fraffin correct? Would they blot this world? They were capable of it. But the natives were so attractive it didn't seem possible they'd be obliterated. They were Chem—wild Chem. But no matter the Primacy's attentions, this place would be overwhelmed. No one presently partaking of its pleasures would have a part in the new order.

Arguments went back and forth in his mind in a pattern much like Ruth's pacing.

Her movement began to anger him. She did this to annoy him, deliberately testing the limits of her power. Kelexel reached beneath his cloak, adjusted the manipulator.

Ruth stopped as though drawn up against a wall. She turned, faced him. "Again?" she asked, her voice flat.

"Take off your robe," he said.

She stood unmoving.

Kelexel exerted more pressure, repeated his command. The manipulator's setting went up . . . up . . . up. . . .

Slowly, woodenly she obeyed. The robe dropped to the silvery piled carpet, leaving her nude. Her flesh appeared suddenly pale. Rippling tremors moved up and down her stomach.

"Turn around," he said.

With the same wooden movement, she obeyed. One of her bare feet caught the emerald belt. Its chain rattled.

"Face me," Kelexel said.

When she'd obeyed, Kelexel released the manipulator's pressure. The tremors stopped moving across her stomach. She took a deep, ragged breath.

How superbly graceful she is, Kelexel thought.

Without taking her gaze from him, Ruth bent, picked up the robe, slipped into it, belted it.

There! she thought. *I've resisted him. I've asserted myself at last. It'll be easier next time.* And she remembered the sodden pressure of the manipulator, the compulsion which had forced her to disrobe. Even in that extremity, she'd felt the sureness that a time would come when she could resist Kelexel's manipulator no matter its pressure. There'd be a limit to the pressure, she knew, but no limit to her growing will to resist. She had only to think of what she'd seen on the pantovive to strengthen that core of resistance.

"You're angry with me," Kelexel said. "Why? I've indulged your every fancy."

For answer, she seated herself at the pantovive's metal webwork, moved its controls. Keys clicked. Instruments hummed.

How deftly she uses her toy, Kelexel thought. *She's been at it more than I suspected. Such practiced sureness! But when has she had time to become this sure? She's never used it in front of me before. I've seen her each rest period. Perhaps time moves at a different rate for mortals. How long to her has she been with me? A quarter of her sun's circuit or maybe a bit more.*

He wondered then how she really felt about the offspring within her body. Primitives felt many things about their bodies, knew many things without recourse to instruments. Some wild sense they had which spoke to them from within. Could the potential offspring be why she was angered?

"Look," Ruth said.

Kelexel sat upright, focused on the pantovive's image stage, the glowing oval where Fraffin's almost-people performed. Figures moved there, the gross wild Chem. Kelexel was suddenly reminded of a comment he'd heard about Fraffin's productions—"Their reverse dollhouse quality." Yes, his *creatures* always managed to seem emotionally as well as physically larger than life.

"These are relatives of mine," Ruth said. "My father's brother and sister. They came out for the trial. This is their motel room."

"Motel?" Kelexel slipped off the bed, crossed to stand beside Ruth.

"Temporary housing," she said. She sat down at the controls.

Kelexel studied the stage. Its bubble of light contained a room of faded maroon. A thin, straw-haired female sat on the edge of a bed at the right. She wore a pink dressing gown. One heavily veined hand dabbed a damp handkerchief at her eyes. Like the furniture, she appeared faded—dull eyes, sagging cheeks. In the general shape of her head and body, she resembled Ruth's father. Kelexel wondered then if Ruth would come to this one day. Surely not. The strange female's eyes peered from deep sockets beneath thin brows.

A man stood facing her, his back to the viewers.

"Now, Claudie," the man said, "there's no sense. . . ."

"I just can't help remembering," she said. A sob in her voice.

Kelexel swallowed. His body drank emotional identification with the creatures in the pantovive. It was uncanny—repellant and at once magnetic. The pantovive's sensi-mesh web projected a cloying sweet emotion from the woman. It was stifling.

"I remember one time on the farm near Marion," she said. "Joey was about three that night we was sitting on the porch after the preacher'd been there to dinner. Paw was wondering out loud how he could get that twelve acres down by the creek."

"He was always wondering that."

"And Joey said he had to go toi-toi."

"That danged outhouse," Grant said.

"Remember them narrow boards across the mud? Joey was still wearing that white suit Ma'd made for him."

"Claudie, what's the use remembering all. . . ."

"You remember that night?"

"Claudie, that was a long time ago."

"I remember it. Joey asked all around for someone to go out with him across them boards, but Paw said for him to git along. What's he scared of?"

"Doggone, Claudie, you sound like Paw sometimes."

"I remember Joey going out there all by hisself—a little white blot like in the dark. Then Paw yipped: 'Joey! Look out for that buck nigger ahint you!' "

"And Joey ran!" Grant said. "I remember."

"And he slipped off into the mud."

"He come back all dirty," Grant said, "I remember." He chuckled.

"And when Paw found out he'd wet hisself, too, he went and got the razor strop." Her voice softened. "Joey was such a little feller."

"Paw was a strict one, all right."

"Funny the things you remember sometimes," she said.

Grant moved across to a window, picked at the maroon drapery. Turning, he revealed his face—the same fine bone structure as Ruth, but with heavy flesh over it. A sharp line crossed his forehead where a hat had been worn, the face dark beneath it, light above. His eyes appeared hidden in shadowed holes. The hand at the drapery was darkly veined.

"This is real dry country," he said. "Nothing ever looks green out here."

"I wonder why he done it?" Claudie asked.

Grant shrugged. "He was a strange one, that Joey."

"Listen to you," she said. "*Was* a strange one. Already talking like he was dead."

"I guess he is, Claudie. Just as good as." He shook his head. "Either dead or committed to an insane asylum. Same thing really when they stick you away like that."

"I heard you talk plenty about what happened when we was kids," she said. "You figure that had anything to do with him going . . . like this?"

"What had anyting to do with it?"

"The way Paw treated him."

Grant found a loose thread in the drapery. He pulled it out, rolled it between his fingers. The sensi-mesh web projected a feeling of long-repressed anger from him.

(Kelexel wondered then why Ruth showed him this scene. He understood in a way the pain she must feel at seeing this, but how could she blame *him* or be angry at *him* for this? What had happened to her parents . . . that'd been Fraffin's doing.)

"That time we went to the county fair to hear the darky singers," Grant said. "In the mule wagon, remember? Joey didn't want to come along. He was mad at Paw for something, but Paw said he was too young to leave at home alone."

"He must've been all of nine then," she said.

Grant went on as though he hadn't heard. "Then when Joey refused to leave the wagon, remember? Paw says: 'Come along, boy. Don't you want to hear them niggers?' And Joey says: 'I guess I'll stay with the mules and wagon.' "

Claudie nodded.

Another thread came out of the drapery into Grant's hand. He said: "I heard you plenty of times when you didn't want to go someplace say: 'Guess I'll stay with the mules and wagon.' We had half the county saying it."

"Joey was like that," she said. "Always wanting to be alone."

Grant's lips formed a harsh smile. "Everything seemed to happen to Joey."

"Was you there when he ran away?"

"Yep. That was after you was married, wasn't it? Paw sold Joey's horse that he'd worked all summer cutting wood to buy from old Poor-John Weeks, Ned Tolliver's brother-in-law."

"Did you see the ruckus?"

"I was right there. Joey called Paw a liar and a cheat and a thief. Paw went to reach for the white oak club, but Joey was quicker. He must've been seventeen then, and strong. He brung that club down on Paw's head like he wanted to kill him. Paw went down like a pole-axed steer. Joey ripped the money Paw'd got for the horse outen his pocket, ran upstairs, packed the gladstone and left."

"That was a terrible thing," she said.

Grant nodded. "Long as I live I'll remember, that

boy standing there on the porch, that bag in his hand
and holding that screen door. Maw was sobbing over
Paw, dabbing at his head with a wet towel. Joey spoke
so low we'd never've heard if we hadn't all been so
scared and quiet. We thought Paw was dead for sure."

" 'I hope I never see any of you ever again,' Joey
says. And he run off."

"He had Paw's temper and that's for sure," Claudie
said.

Ruth slapped the pantovive cutoff. The images
faded. She turned, her face composed and blank from
the pressures of the manipulator, but there were tear
stains down her cheeks.

"I must know something," she said. "Did you Chem
do that to my father? Did you . . . make him that
way?"

Kelexel recalled Fraffin boasting how the killer had
been *prepared* . . . boasting and explaining how an Investigator from the Primacy stood no chance to escape
the traps of this world. But why waste concern over a
few suborders demeaned and shaped to Chem needs?
Precisely because they were *not* suborders. They were
wild Chem.

"You did, I see," Ruth said. "I suspected it from
what you've told me."

Am I so transparent to her? Kelexel asked himself.
*How did she know that? What strange powers do these
natives have?*

He covered his confusion with a shrug.

"I wish you could die," Ruth said. "I want you to
die."

Despite the manipulator's pressure on her, Ruth
could feel rage deep inside her, remote but distinct, a
burning and smoldering anger that made her want to
reach out and waste her fingernails clawing at this
Chem's impervious skin.

Ruth's voice had come out so level and flat that
Kelexel found he'd heard the words and almost passed
over them before he absorbed their meaning. Die! She
wished him dead! He recoiled. What a boorish, outrageous thing for her to say!

"I am a Chem," he said. "How dare you say such a thing to a Chem?"

"You really don't know, do you?" she asked.

"I've smiled upon you, brought you into my society," he said. "Is this your gratitude?" Kelexel slipped off the bed, crossed the room.

She glanced around her prison room, focused on his face—the silvery skin dull and metallic, the features drawn into a sharp frown of disdain. Kelexel's position standing beside her chair put him only slightly above her and she could see the dark hairs quivering in his nostrils as he breathed.

"I almost pity you," she said.

Kelexel swallowed. *Pity?* Her reaction was unnerving. He looked down at his hands, was surprised to find them clasped tightly together. *Pity?* Slowly, he separated his fingers, noting how the nails were getting that foggy warning look, the reaction from breeding. Reproducing itself, his body had set the clock of flesh ticking. Rejuvenation was needed, and that soon. Was this why she pitied him, because he'd delayed his rejuvenation? No; she couldn't know of the Chem subservience to the Rejuvenators.

Delay . . . delay . . . why am I delaying? Kelexel wondered.

Suddenly, he marveled at himself—his own bravery and daring. He'd let himself go far beyond the point where other Chem went racing for the Rejuvenators. He'd done this thing almost deliberately, he knew, toying with sensations of mortality. What other Chem would've dared. They were cowards all! He was almost like Ruth in this. Almost mortal! And here she railed at him! She didn't understand. How could she, poor creature?

A wave of self-pity washed through him. How could anyone understand this? Who even knew? His fellow Chem would all assume he'd availed himself of a Rejuvenator when he'd needed it. No one understood.

Kelexel hesitated on the verge of telling Ruth this daring thing he'd done, but he remembered her words. She wished him dead.

"How can I show you?" Ruth asked. Again, she

turned to the pantovive, adjusted its controls. This disgusting machine, product of the disgusting Chem, was suddenly very important to her. It was the most vital thing in her life at this moment to show Kelexel why she nurtured such a seed of violent hate toward him. "Look," she said.

Within the pantovive's bubble of light there appeared a long room with a high desk at one end, rows of benches below it set off behind a rail, tables, another railed-off section on the right with twelve natives seated in it in various poses of boredom. The side walls held spaced Grecian columns separated by dark wood paneling and tall windows. Morning sunlight poured in the windows. Behind the high desk sat a round ball of a man in black robes, bald pod of head bent forward into the light.

Kelexel found he recognized some of the natives seated at the tables below the high desk. There was the squat figure of Joe Murphey, Ruth's parent, and there was Bondelli, the legal expert he'd seen in Fraffin's story rushes—narrow face, black hair combed back in beetle wings. In chairs immediately behind the railing there were the witch doctors, Whelye and Thurlow.

Thurlow interested Kelexel. Why had she chosen a scene containing that native male? Was it true that she'd have mated with this creature?

"That's Judge Grimm," Ruth said, indicating the man in the black robes. "I . . . I went to school with his daughter. Do you know that? I've . . . been in his home."

Kelexel heard the sounds of distress in her voice, considered a higher setting on the manipulator, decided against it. That might introduce too much inhibition for her to continue. He found himself intensely curious now as to what Ruth was doing. What could her motives be?

"The man with the cane there at the left, at that table, that's Paret, the District Attorney," Ruth said. "His wife and my mother were in the same garden club."

Kelexel looked at the native she'd indicated. There was a look of solidness and integrity about him.

Iron gray hair topped a squarish head. The hair made a straight line across his forehead and was trimmed closely above prominent ears. The chin had a forward thrust. The mouth was a prim, neat modulation on the way to a solid nose. The brows were bushy brown ovals above blue eyes. At their outer edges, the eyes made a slight downward slant accented by deep creases.

The cane leaned against the table beside his chair. Now and again, Paret touched its knobbed top.

Something important appeared to be happening in this room now. Ruth turned up the sound and there came a noise of coughing from the ranked spectators, a hissing sound as papers were shuffled.

Kelexel leaned forward, a hand on the back of Ruth's chair, staring as Thurlow arose and went to a chair beside the high desk. There was a brief religious rite involving truthfulness and Thurlow was seated, the legal expert, Bondelli, standing below him.

Kelexel studied Thurlow—the wide forehead, the dark hair. Without the manipulator, would Ruth prefer this creature? Thurlow gave the impression of crouching behind his dark glasses. There was an aura of shifting uneasiness about him. He was refusing to look in a particular place. It came over Kelexel that Thurlow was avoiding Fraffin's shooting crew in this scene. He was aware of the Chem! Of course! He was immune.

A sense of duty returned momentarily to Kelexel then. He felt shame, guilt. And he knew quite suddenly why he hadn't gone to one of the storyship's Rejuvenators. Once he did that, he'd be committed finally to Fraffin's trap. He'd be one of them, owned by Fraffin as certainly as any native of this world. As long as he put it off, Kelexel knew he was just that much free of Fraffin. It was only a matter of time, though.

Bondelli was speaking to Thurlow now and it seemed a tired, useless little scene. Kelexel wondered at his reaction.

"Now, Dr. Thurlow," Bondelli said, "you've enumerated the points this defendant has in common with other insane killers. What else leads you to the conclusion that he is in fact insane?"

"I was attracted to the recurrence of the number seven," Thurlow said. "Seven blows with the sword. He told the arresting officers he'd be out in seven minutes."

"Is this important?"

"Seven has religious significance: the Lord made the world in seven days, and so on. It's the kind of thing you find dominant in the actions of the insane."

"Did you, Dr. Thurlow, examine this defendant some months ago?"

"Yes, sir."

"Under what circumstances?"

Kelexel glanced at Ruth, noted with a sense of shock the tears streaming down her cheeks. He looked at the manipulator's setting and began to understand how profound her emotions must be.

"Mr. Murphey had turned in a false fire alarm," Thurlow said. "He was identified and arrested. I was called in as court psychologist."

"Why?"

"False fire alarms are not a thing to be disregarded, especially when turned in by a man well along in his adult years."

"This is why you were called in?"

"No—that was routine, more or less."

"But what's the significance of the false fire alarm?"

"It's sexual, basically. This incident occurred at about the time this defendant first complained of sexual impotency. These two things, taken together, paint a very disturbing psychological picture."

"How is that?"

"Well, he also displayed an almost complete lack of warmth in his nature. It was a failing in those things we usually refer to as *kindly*. He produced Rorschach responses at that time which were almost completely lacking in those elements we refer to as *alive*. In other words, his outlook was centered on death. I took all of those things into consideration: a cold nature centered on death plus sexual disturbance."

Kelexel stared at the figure on the pantovive's stage. Who was he talking about? Cold, centered on death, sexually disturbed. Kelexel glanced at the figure of Murphey. The defendant sat huddled over his table, eyes downcast.

Bondelli ran a finger along his mustache, glanced at a note in his hand.

"What was the substance of your report to the Probation Department, doctor?" Bondelli asked. As he spoke, he looked at Judge Grimm.

"I warned them that unless he changed his ways radically, this man was headed for a psychotic break."

Still without looking at Thurlow, Bondelli asked: "And would you define psychotic break, doctor?"

"By example—a sword slaying of a loved one using violence and wild passion is a psychotic break."

Judge Grimm scribbled on a piece of paper in front of him. A woman juror on the far right frowned at Bondelli.

"You predicted this crime?" Bondelli asked.

"In a real sense—yes."

The District Attorney was watching the jury. He shook his head slowly, leaned over to whisper to an aide.

"Was any action taken on your report?" Bondelli asked.

"To my knowledge, none."

"Well, why not?"

"Perhaps many of those who saw the report weren't aware of the dangers involved in the terms."

"Did you attempt to impress the sense of danger upon anyone?"

"I explained my worries to several members of the Probation Department."

"And still no action was taken?"

"They said that surely Mr. Murphey, an important member of the community, couldn't be dangerous, that possibly I was mistaken."

"I see. Did you make any personal effort to help this defendant?"

"I attempted to interest him in religion."

"Without success?"

"That's right."

"Have you examined defendant recently?"

"Last Wednesday—which was my second examination of him since he was arrested."

"And what did you find?"

"He's suffering from a condition I'd define as a paranoic state."

"Could he have known the nature and consequences of his act?"

"No, sir. His mental condition would've been such as to override any considerations of law or morality."

Bondelli turned away, stared for a long moment at the District Attorney, then: "That is all, doctor."

The District Attorney passed a finger across the squared-off hairline of his forehead, studied his notes on the testimony.

Kelexel, absorbed in the intricacies of the scene, nodded to himself. The natives obviously had a rudimentary legal system and sense of justice, but it was all very crude. Still, it reminded him of his own guilt. Could that be why Ruth showed him this? he wondered. Was she saying: "You, too, could be punished"? A paroxysm of shame convulsed him then. He felt that somehow Ruth had put him on trial here, placed him by proxy in that room of judgment which the pantovive reproduced. He suddenly identified with her father, sharing the native's emotion through the pantovive's sensi-mesh web.

And Murphey was seated in silent rage, the emotion directed with violent intensity against Thurlow who still sat in the witness chair.

That immune must be destroyed! Kelexel thought.

The pantovive's image focus shifted slightly, centered on the District Attorney. Paret arose, limped to a position below Thurlow, leaned on the cane. Paret's narrow mouth was held in a thin look of primness, but anger smoldered from the eyes.

"Mr. Thurlow," he said, pointedly withholding the title of doctor. "Am I correct in assuming that, in your opinion, defendant was incapable of determining right from wrong on the night he killed his wife?"

Thurlow removed his glasses. His eyes appeared

gray and defenseless without them. He wiped the lenses, replaced them, dropped his hands to his lap. "Yes, sir."

"And the kinds of tests you administered, were they generally the same kinds as were administered to this defendant by Dr. Whelye and those who agreed with him?"

"Essentially the same—inkblot, wool sorting, various other shifting tests."

Paret consulted his notes. "You've heard Dr. Whelye testify that defendant was legally and medically sane at the time of this crime?"

"I heard that testimony, sir."

"You're aware that Dr. Whelye is former police psychiatrist for the city of Los Angeles and served in the Army medical corps at the Nuremberg trials?"

"I'm aware of Dr. Whelye's qualifications." There was a lonely, defensive quality to Thurlow's voice that brought a twinge of sympathy to Kelexel as he watched.

"You see what they're doing to him?" Ruth asked.

"What does it matter?" Kelexel asked. But even as he spoke, Kelexel realized that Thurlow's fate mattered enormously. And this was precisely because Thurlow, even though he was being destroyed and knew it, was sticking to his principles. There was no doubt that Murphey was insane. He'd been driven insane by Fraffin—for a purpose.

I was that purpose, Kelexel thought.

"Then you have heard," Paret said, "this expert *medical* testimony rule out any element of organic brain damage in this case? You've heard these qualified *medical* men testify that defendant shows no manic tendencies, that he does not now suffer and never has suffered from a condition which could be legally described as insanity?"

"Yes, sir."

"Then you can explain why you've arrived at a conflicting opinion to these qualified *medical* men?"

Thurlow uncrossed his legs, planted both feet firmly on the floor. He put his hands on the arms of his chair, leaned forward. "That's quite simple, sir. Ability in psychiatry and psychology is usually judged by results. In this case, I stake my claim to a different viewpoint on the fact that I *predicted* this crime."

Anger darkened Paret's face.

Kelexel heard Ruth whispering: "Andy, oh, Andy . . . oh, Andy. . . ." Her voice sent a sudden pain through Kelexel's breast and he hissed: "Be silent!"

Again, Paret consulted his notes, then: "You're a psychologist, not a psychiatrist, is that correct?"

"I'm a clinical psychologist."

"What's the difference between a psychologist and a psychiatrist?"

"A psychologist is a specialist in human behavior who does not have a medical degree. The. . . ."

"And you disagree with men who *do* have medical degrees?"

"As I said previously. . . ."

"Ah, yes, your so-called prediction. I've read that report, Mr. Thurlow, and I'd like to ask you this: Is it not true that your probation report was couched in language which might be translated several ways—that it was, in a word, ambiguous?"

"It might be considered ambiguous only by someone who was unfamiliar with the term *psychotic break*."

"Ahhh, and what is a psychotic break?"

"An extremely dangerous break with reality which can lead to acts of violence such as that being considered here."

"But if there'd been no crime, if this defendant had recovered from the alleged illness which you say he has, could your probation report have been construed as predicting *that?*"

"Not without an explanation of *why* he recovered."

"Let me ask this, then: Can violence have no other explanation except psychosis?"

"Certainly it can, but. . . ."

"Is it not true that psychosis is a disputed term?"

"There are differences of opinion."

"Differences such as are being evidenced here?"

"Yes."

"And any given act of violence may be caused by things other than a psychosis?"

"Of course." Thurlow shook his head. "But in a delusionary system. . . ."

"Delusionary?" Paret snapped at the word. "What is delusion, Mr. Thurlow?"

"Delusion? That's a kind of inner ineptness at dealing with reality."

"Reality," Paret said. And again: "Reality. Tell me, Mr. Thurlow, do you believe the defendant's accusations against his wife?"

"I do not!"

"But if defendant's accusations were real, would that change your opinion, sir, about his *delusionary* system?"

"My opinion is based on. . . ."

"Yes or no, Mr. Thurlow! Answer the question!"

"I *am* answering it!" Thurlow pushed himself back in his chair, took a deep breath. "You're trying to blacken the reputation of a defenseless. . . ."

"Mr. Thurlow! My questions are aimed at whether defendant's accusations are reasonable in the light of all the evidence. I agree they cannot be proved or disproved with the principal dead, but are the accusations reasonable?"

Thurlow swallowed, then: "Was it reasonable to kill, sir?"

Paret's face darkened. His voice came out low, deadly: "It's time we quit playing with words, Mr. Thurlow. Will you tell the court, please, if you have any other relationship with the defendant's family than that of . . . psychologist?"

Thurlow's knuckles went white as he gripped the chair arm. "What do you mean?" he asked.

"Were you not at one time engaged to defendant's daughter?"

Thurlow nodded mutely.

"Speak up," Paret said. "Were you?"

"Yes."

At the defense table, Bondelli stood up, glared at Paret, looked up at the judge. "Your honor, I object. This line of questioning is not relevant."

Slowly, Paret swiveled. He leaned heavily on his cane, said: "Your honor, the jury has the right to know *all* the factors which have guided this *expert* witness in arriving at his opinion."

"What is your intention?" Judge Grimm asked. He looked over Paret's head at the jury.

"Defendant's daughter is not available for testimony, your honor. She is missing under mysterious circumstances attendant upon the death of her husband. This *expert* witness was in the immediate vicinity when the husband. . . ."

"Your honor, I object!" Bondelli pounded a fist on the table.

Judge Grimm pursed his lips. He glanced down at Thurlow's profile, then at Paret. "What I say now I do not say as approval or as disapproval of Dr. Thurlow's present testimony. But I will state by way of accepting his qualifications that he is psychologist for this court. As such, he may present opinions in disagreement with the opinions of other qualified witnesses. This is the privilege of expert testimony. It is up to the jury to decide which experts it will accept as being the most reliable. The jury may arrive at such decision strictly on the expert qualifications of the witnesses. Objection sustained."

Paret shrugged. He limped a step closer to Thurlow, appeared about to speak, hesitated, then: "Very well. No more questions."

"Witness may stand down," the judge said.

As the scene began to fade under Ruth's manipulation of the pantovive, Kelexel focused on Joe Murphey. The defendant was smiling, a sly, secretive smile.

Kelexel nodded, matched that smile. Nothing was entirely lost when even the victims could share amusement at their predicament.

Ruth turned, saw the smile on Kelexel's face. In her flat, controlled voice, she said: "God damn you for every second of your goddamn' eternity."

Kelexel blinked.

"You're as crazy as my father," she said. "Andy's describing you when he talks about my father." She whirled back to the pantovive. "See yourself!"

Kelexel took a deep, shivering breath. The pantovive screeched as Ruth twisted its controls and rapped keys.

He wanted to jerk her away from the machine, fearful of what she might show him. *See myself?* he wondered. It was a terrifying thought. A Chem did not see himself in the pantovive!

The bubble of light on the image stage became Bondelli's law office, the big desk, glass-fronted bookcases shielding the mud-red backs of law books with their gold lettering. Bondelli sat behind the desk, a pencil in his right hand. He pushed the pencil point down through his fingers, repeated the action with the eraser against the desk. The eraser left little rubber smudges on the polished surface.

Thurlow sat across from him behind a scattering of papers. He clutched his heavy glasses like a lecturer's pointer in his left hand, waving them as he spoke.

"The delusional system is like a mask," Thurlow said. Vertical cords smoothed and reappeared in his neck as he gestured. "Behind that mask, Murphey *wants* to be found sane even though he knows that this condemns him to death."

"It's not logical," Bondelli muttered.

"And if it isn't logical it's the most difficult thing there is to prove," Thurlow said. "This is hard to put into words that can be understood by people who haven't had long familiarity with such things. But if Murphey's delusional system were shattered, if we penetrated it, broke it down, this could be compared to what it would be like for an ordinary person to awaken one morning and find his bed different from the one he thought he went to sleep in, the room different, a different woman saying, 'I'm your wife!', unfamiliar youngsters claiming him as father. He'd be overwhelmed, his whole concept of his life destroyed."

"Total unreality," Bondelli whispered.

"Reality from the standpoint of an objective observer isn't important here," Thurlow said. "As long as Murphey maintains the delusional system he saves himself from the psychological equivalent of annihilation. That, of course, is the fear of death."

"Fear of death?" Bondelli appeared puzzled. "But that's what faces him if. . . ."

"There're two kinds of death here. Murphey has far

less fear for real death in the gas chamber than he has for the kind of death he'd experience in the collapse of his delusional world."

"But can't he *see* the difference?"

"No."

"That's crazy!"

Thurlow appeared surprised. "Isn't that what we've been saying?"

Bondelli dropped the pencil onto the desk with a sharp click. "And what happens if he's judged sane?"

"He'd be convinced he controlled this one last piece of his misfortune. To him, insanity means loss of control. It means he's not the all great, all powerful person in control of his own destiny. If he controls even his own death, this is grandeur—a delusion of grandeur."

"This isn't something you can prove in a court of law," Bondelli said.

"Especially not in this community and not right now," Thurlow said. "That's what I've been trying to tell you from the beginning. You know Vauntman, my neighbor to the south? My walnut tree had a limb overhanging his yard. I've always let him have the nuts off it. We made a joke about it. Last night he sawed that limb off and threw it in my yard—because I'm testifying for Murphey's defense."

"That's insane!"

"Right now insanity is the norm," Thurlow said. He shook his head. "Vauntman's perfectly normal under most circumstances. But this Murphey thing's a sex crime and it's stirred up a rat's nest of unconscious content—guilt, fear, shame—that people aren't equipped to handle. Vauntman's just one isolated symptom. The whole community's undergoing a kind of psychotic break."

Thurlow put on his dark glasses, turned, stared directly out of the pantovive.

"The whole community," he whispered.

Ruth reached out like a blind person, shut off the pantovive. As the stage darkened, Thurlow still stared out at her, *Goodbye, Andy,* she thought. *Dear Andy. Destroyed Andy. I'll never see you again.*

Abruptly, Kelexel whirled away, strode across the

room. He turned there, stared at Ruth's back, cursing the day he'd first seen her. *In the name of Silence!* he thought. *Why did I succumb to her?*

Thurlow's words still rang in his ears—*Grandeur! Delusion! Death!*

What was it about these natives that locked on the mind and senses, refusing to let go? A rage such as he'd never before experienced flooded through Kelexel then.

How dare she say I am like her father?

How dare she harbor one thought for her puny native lover when she has me?

An odd rasping sound was coming from Ruth. Her shoulders trembled and shook. Kelexel realized she was sobbing despite the manipulator's suppression. The realization fed his rage.

Slowly, she turned in the pantovive's chair, stared at him. Strange lines of grief wavered across her face. "Live forever!" she hissed. "And every day you live, I hope your crime gnaws at you!" The hate was stark in her eyes.

A sense of dismay shook Kelexel. *How can she know of my crime?* he asked himself.

But rage was there to support him.

She was contaminated by that immune! he thought. *Let her see what a Chem can do to her lover, then!*

With a vicious movement, Kelexel twisted the manipulator's controls beneath his tunic. The pressure, building up abruptly, jerked Ruth backward into her chair, stiffened her body then relaxed it. She slumped into unconsciousness.

17

FRAFFIN SWEPT ONTO THE LANDING PLATFORM WITH long, angry strides, his cloak whipping about his bowed legs. The sea shone like dark green crystals beyond the spider lines of the enclosing field. A file of ten flitters stood ready along the gray ramp, prepared to debark on his orders, checking the status of their "lovely little war." Perhaps it could still be saved. There was a biting smell of damp ozone in the air. It made the guardian layers of Fraffin's skin crawl in a protective reflex.

He could sense the planet flowering for him up there, spewing forth story after story in such a profusion as it had never done before. But if the report on Kelexel were true. . . . It couldn't be true. Logic said it couldn't be true.

Fraffin slowed his stride as he approached traffic control, the yellow bubble eye with Lutt, his Master-of-Craft, personally in charge. The squat, solid body of the crewman imparted a feeling of reassurance to Fraffin. Lutt's square face was bent over the yellow eye.

There was a crafty look to Lutt, though, and Fraffin suddenly remembered Cato saying: "Fear kings whose slaves are crafty." Ah, there'd been a native to admire—Cato. And Fraffin recalled Cato's Carthaginian enemies, the two kings looking down from Citadel-Byrsa onto the inner harbor of Corthon. "Proper sacrifice, right thinking, the best gods—those bring victory." Cato had said that, too.

But Cato was dead, his life whirled up in the crazy time-blur that was a Chem's memory. He was dead and the two kings were dead.

Surely the report on Kelexel is wrong, Fraffin thought.

A waiting flitter crewman signaled Lutt. The Master-of-Craft straightened, turned to face Fraffin. An alert air of caution in the man destroyed all illusion of reassurance.

He looks a little like Cato, Fraffin thought as he stopped three paces from Lutt. *The same sort of bone structure in the face. Ah, we've bred much of ourselves into this place.* Fraffin pulled his cloak around him, aware of a sudden chill in the air.

"Honored director," Lutt said. How warily he spoke!

"I've just heard a disturbing report about the Investigator," Fraffin said.

"The Investigator?"

"Kelexel, you oaf!"

Lutt's tongue darted out and across his lips. He glanced left, right, returned his attention to Fraffin. "He ... he said he had your permission to ... he had the native female with him in a tagalong floater ... she ... what is wrong?"

Fraffin took a moment to compose himself. There was a slackdrum throbbing through every micro-instant that lay immersed in his being. This planet and its creatures! The erection/detumescence of each instant he'd shared with them lay on his awareness with scalding pressure. He felt like a bivalve at the tide-edge of the universe. History was collapsing within him and he could only remember the ages of his crime.

"The Investigator is gone then?" Fraffin asked, and he was proud of how calmly his voice emerged.

"Just a short trip," Lutt whispered. "He said just a short trip." Lutt nodded, a swift, jerking motion full of nervousness. "I . . . everyone said the Investigator'd been snared. He had the female with him. She was unconscious!" Lutt pounced on this revelation as though it were a most important discovery. "The native female was unconscious in the flitter!" A sly smile twitched Lutt's mouth. "The better to control her, he said."

Fraffin spoke through a dry mouth: "Did he say where?"

"Planetside," Lutt hooked a thumb upward.

Fraffin's eyes followed the motion, noting the warty skin, his mind filled with wonder that such a casual gesture could carry such a weight of terrifying possibilities.

"In the needleship?" Fraffin asked.

"He said he was more familiar with its controls," Lutt said.

There was a veil of fear over Lutt's eyes now. The Director's bland voice and appearance couldn't conceal the slashing purpose of these questions—and there'd already been one flash of anger.

"He assured me he had your approval," Lutt rasped. "He said it was part of his training when he gets his own. . . ." The glare in Fraffin's eyes stopped him, then: "He said the female would enjoy it."

"But she was unconscious," Fraffin said.

Lutt's head bobbed in affirmation.

Why was she unconscious? Fraffin wondered. Hope began to grow in him. *What can he do? We own him! I was a fool to panic.*

Beside Lutt, the eye of the traffic control selector shifted from yellow to red, blinked twice for override. The instrument emitted a harsh buzzing and projected Ynvic's round face onto the air in front of them. The shipsurgeon's features were drawn into a tight mask of worry. Her eyes stared fixedly at Fraffin.

"There you are!" she snapped. Her gaze darted to Lutt, to the platform background, returned to Fraffin. "Has he gone?"

"And taken the female with him," Fraffin said.

"He's not been rejuvenated!" Ynvic blurted.

It took a long minute for Fraffin to find his voice. "But all the others . . . he . . . you. . . ." Again, he felt the distant slackdrum..

"Yes, all the others went immediately to the Rejuvenator," Ynvic agreed. "So I assumed this one'd been handled by an assistant or that Kelexel had taken care of it himself. You do!" A rasp of feral anger touched her voice. "Who'd think otherwise? But there's not a trace of him in Master Records. He's not been rejuvenated!"

Fraffin swallowed in a dry throat. This was unthinkable! He felt himself go deathly still as though listening for the passage of suns and moons and planets his kind had all but forgotten. Not rejuvenated! The time . . . the time. . . . His voice came out a husky whisper: "It's been at least. . . ."

"One of my assistants saw him with the female just a short while ago and alerted me," Ynvic said. "Kelexel shows obvious signs of deterioration."

Fraffin found it difficult to breathe. His chest ached. Not rejuvenated! If Kelexel destroyed all traces of the female. . . . But he couldn't! The storyship had a complete record of the liasion with the native. But if Kelexel destroyed her. . . .

Lutt tugged at Fraffin's coat.

In a rage, Fraffin whirled on him: "What do you want?"

Lutt ducked backward, peered up at Fraffin. "Honored director, the intercom. . . ." Lutt touched the pickup instrument imbedded in the bone of his neck. "Kelexel's needleship has been seen planetside."

"Where?"

"In the home region of the female."

"Do they still see him?"

Fraffin held his breath.

Lutt listened a moment, shook his head. "The ship was seen to pass without shields. One who saw it inquired about this breach of security. He no longer has the ship in view."

Planetside! Fraffin thought.

"You will drop every other activity!" he rasped. "You will order out every pilot and vehicle. That ship must be found! It must be found!"

"But . . . what do we do when we find it?"

"The female," Ynvic said.

Fraffin glanced at the disembodied face projected above the traffic control selector, returned his attention to Lutt. "Yes, the female. You'll take her into custody and return her here. She's our property. We'll have an understanding with this Kelexel. No nonsense, you hear? Bring her to me."

"If I can, honored director."

"You had better find a way," Fraffin said.

18

THURLOW AWOKE AT THE FIRST CLICK OF THE ALARM clock, turned it off before it rang. He sat up in bed, fighting a deep reluctance to face this day. It'd be hellish at the hospital, he knew. Whelye was putting on the pressure and would keep it up until. . . . Thurlow took a deep sighing breath. When it got bad enough, he knew he'd quit.

The community was helping him to this decision—crank letters, vicious phone calls. He was a pariah.

The professionals were an odd contrast—Paret and old Judge Victor Venning Grimm among them. What they did in court and what they did outside of court appeared to be held in separate, carefully insulated compartments.

"It'll blow over," Grimm had said. "Give it time."

And Paret: "Well, Andy, you win some, you lose some."

Thurlow wondered if they had any but detached emotions about Murphey's death. Paret had been invited to the execution, and the courthouse grapevine had said he debated going. Good sense had prevailed, though. His advisors had warned against his appearing vindictive.

Why did I go? Thurlow asked himself. *Did I want to extract the last measure of personal pain from this?*

But he knew why he'd gone, meekly accepting the condemned man's wry invitation to "Watch me die." It'd been the lure of his own personal hallucination: Would the watchers be there, too, in their hovering craft?

They . . . or the illusion had been there.

Are they real? Are they real? his mind pleaded.

Then: *Ruth, where are you?* He felt that if she could only return with a reasonable explanation for her disappearance, the hallucinations would go.

His thoughts veered back to the execution. It would take more than one long weekend to erase that memory. Recollection of the sounds bothered him—the clang of metal against metal, the whisper-shuffling of feet as the guards came into the execution area with Murphey.

The memory of the condemned man's glazed eyes lay across Thurlow's vision. Murphey had lost some of his dumpiness. The prison suit hung slackly on him. He walked with a heavy, dragging limp. Ahead of him walked a black-robed priest chanting in a sonorous voice that concealed an underlying whine.

In his mind, Thurlow watched them pass, feeling all the spectators caught up abruptly in a spasm of silence. Every eye turned then to the executioner. He looked like a drygoods clerk, tall, bland-faced, efficient—standing there beside the rubber-sealed door into the little green room with its eyeless portholes.

The executioner took one of Murphey's arms, helped him over the hatch sill. One guard and the priest followed. Thurlow was in a line to look directly through the hatchway and hear their conversation.

The guard passed a strap over Murphey's left arm, told him to sit farther back in the chair. "Put your hand here, Joe. A little farther this way." The guard cinched the strap. "Does that strap hurt?"

Murphey shook his head. His eyes remained glazed, a trapped animal look in them.

The executioner looked at the guard, said: "Al, why don't you stay in here and hold his hand?"

In that instant, Murphey came out of the depths to shatter Thurlow, forcing him to turn away. "You best stay with the mules and wagon," Murphey said.

It was a phrase Thurlow had heard Ruth use . . . many times, one of those odd family expressions that meant something special to the inner circle of intimates. Hearing Murphey use it then had forged a link between father and daughter that nothing could break.

All else was anticlimax.

Remembering that moment, Thurlow sighed, swung his feet out of the bed onto the cold floor. He pulled on his slippers, donned a robe and crossed to the window. There, he stood staring at the view which had brought his father to buy this house twenty-five years before.

The morning light hurt his eyes and they began to water. Thurlow took up his dark glasses from the bedstand, slipped them on, lightened the setting to just below the pain threshold.

The valley had its usual morning overcast, the redwood fog that would burn off sometime around eleven. Two ravens sat perched in the branches of a live oak below him calling to unseen companions. A drop of condensation spilled from an acacia leaf directly beneath the window.

Beyond the tree there was motion. Thurlow turned toward it, saw a cigar-shaped object about thirty feet long lift into view. It drifted across the top of the oak, scattering the ravens. They flapped away, croaking with harsh dissonance.

They see it! Thurlow told himself. *It's real!*

Abruptly, the thing launched itself across the sky to his left, lanced into the overcast. Behind it came a covey of spheres and discs.

All were swallowed by the clouds.

Into the shocked stillness with which Thurlow enveloped himself there came a rasping voice: "You are the native, Thurlow."

Thurlow whirled to see an apparition in his bedroom doorway—a squat, bowlegged figure in a green cape and leotards, square face, dark hair, silvery skin, a wide gash of mouth. The creature's eyes burned feverishly under pronounced brows.

The mouth moved, and again came that harsh, resonant voice: "I am Kelexel." The English was clear, clipped.

Thurlow stared. *A dwarf?* he asked himself. *A lunatic?* He found his mind jammed with questions.

Kelexel glanced out the window behind Thurlow. It had been faintly amusing to watch Fraffin's pack go hounding after the empty needleship. The programmed automatic course couldn't elude the pursuers forever, of course, but by the time they caught it, all would have been accomplished here. There'd be no bringing back the dead.

Fraffin would have to face that . . . and his crime.

Resurgent pride firmed Kelexel's will. He frowned at Thurlow, thinking: *I know my duty.* Ruth would waken soon, he knew, and come to their voices. When she did, she could watch a supreme triumph. *She'll be proud that a Chem smiled upon her,* he thought.

"I have watched you, witch doctor," Kelexel said.

A thought flickered through Thurlow's mind: *Is this some weird psychotic come to kill me because of my testimony?*

"How did you get into my house?" Thurlow demanded.

"For a Chem it was simplicity," Kelexel said.

Thurlow had the sudden nightmare feeling that this creature might be connected with the objects that had flown into the clouds, with the watchers who. . . . *What is a Chem?* he wondered.

"How have you watched me?" Thurlow asked.

"Your antics have been captured in . . . in a. . . ." Kelexel waved a knob-knuckled hand in exasperation. It was so difficult to communicate with these creatures. ". . . in a thing like your movies," he concluded. "It's much more, of course—a sensation transcript that works directly on the audience by empathic stimulation."

Thurlow cleared his throat. The words made only the vaguest sense, but his feelings of disquiet increased. His voice came out hoarsely: "Something new, no doubt."

"New?" Kelexel chuckled. "Older than your galaxy."

He must be a crank, Thurlow reassured himself. *Why do they always pick on psychologists?*

But he remembered the ravens. No blandishment of logic could erase the fact that the ravens had seen these . . . things too. Again, he asked himself: *What is a Chem?*

"You don't believe me," Kelexel said. "You don't *want* to believe me." He could feel relaxation seep through his body like a warm drink. Ahh, this was amusing. He saw the fascination Fraffin's people must have known once intimidating these creatures. The anger and jealousy he had directed against Thurlow began to dissipate.

Thurlow swallowed. His reason directed him into outrageous channels of thought. "If I believed you," he said, "I'd have to infer you were . . . well, some kind of. . . ."

"Someone from another world?"

"Yes."

Kelexel laughed. "The things I could do! I could frighten you into a stupor like that!" He snapped his fingers.

It was a solidly human gesture from this inhuman looking person. Thurlow saw it and took a deep breath. He gave a closer examination to his caller's clothes: the cape, the leotards. He looked at the oddly high-positioned ears. *The cape could've come from a theatrical outfitter,* he thought. *He looks like a dwarf Bela Lugosi. Can't be over four feet tall.*

A near panic fear of his visitor shot through Thurlow then. "Why're you here?" he demanded.

Why am I here? For a moment no logical reason came to Kelexel's mind. He thought of Ruth unconscious on the tagalong in the other room. This Thurlow might've been her mate. A pang of jealousy gripped Kelexel.

"Perhaps I came to put you in your place," he said. "Perhaps I'll take you to my ship far above your silly planet and show you what an unimportant speck it is."

I must humor him, Thurlow thought. He said: "Let's grant this isn't a joke in bad taste and you're. . . ."

"You don't tell a Chem he has bad taste," Kelexel said.

Thurlow heard the violence in Kelexel's voice. By an effort of conscious will, he paced his breathing to an even rhythm, stared at the intruder. *Could this be the reason Ruth is gone?* he wondered. *Is this one of the creatures who took her, who've been spying on me, who watched poor Joe Murphey die, who. . . .*

"I've broken the most important laws of my society

to come here," Kelexel said. "It astonishes me what I've done."

Thurlow took off his glasses, found a handkerchief on his dresser, polished the lenses, returned them to his nose. *I must keep him talking,* he thought. *As long as he continues to talk, he's venting his violence.*

"What is a Chem?" Thurlow asked.

"Good," Kelexel said. "You have normal curiosity." He began to explain the Chem in broad outline, their power, their immortality, their storyships.

Still no mention of Ruth. Thurlow wondered if he dared ask about her.

"Why have you come to me?" he asked. "What if I told about you?"

"Perhaps you'll not be able to tell about us," Kelexel said. "And who'd believe you if you did?"

Thurlow focused on the threat. Granting that this Kelexel was who he said he was, then here was profound danger. Who could stand against such a creature. Thurlow suddenly saw himself as a Sandwich Islander facing iron cannon.

"Why're you here?" he repeated.

Annoying question! Kelexel thought. A momentary confusion overcame him. Why was the witch doctor so persistent? But he was a witch doctor, a primitive, and perhaps knowledgeable in mysterious ways. "You may know things helpful to me," he said.

"Helpful? If you come from such an advanced civilization that you. . . ."

"I will question you and dispute with you," Kelexel said. "Perhaps something will emerge."

Why is he here? Thurlow asked himself. *If he's what he says he is . . . why?* Bits of Kelexel's phrases sorted themselves through Thurlow's awareness. *Immortal. Storyships. Search for amusement. Nemesis boredom. Immortal. Immortal. Immortal. . . Boredom!*

Thurlow's stare began to rasp on Kelexel. "You doubt your sanity, eh?" Kelexel asked.

"Is that why you're here?" Thurlow asked. "Because you doubt your sanity?" It was the wrong thing to say and Thurlow knew it the moment the words were out of his mouth.

"How dare you?" Kelexel demanded. "*My* civilization monitors the sanity of all its members. The order-
liness of our neural content is insured by the original
setting to Tiggywaugh's web when the infant receives the
gift of immortality."

"Tiggy . . . Tiggywaugh's web?" Thurlow asked. "A
. . . a mechanical device?"

"Mechanical? Well . . . yes."

Great heavens! Thurlow thought. *Is he here to pro-
mote some wild psychoanalytic machine? Is this just a
promotion scheme?*

"The web links all Chem," Kelexel said. "We're the
daoine-sithe, you understand? The many who are one.
This gives us insights you couldn't imagine, poor creature. It makes the storyships possible. You have nothing like it and you're blind."

Thurlow suppressed a feeling of outrage. *A mechanical device!* Didn't the poor fool realize he was talking to
a psychologist? Thurlow put aside anger, knowing he
couldn't afford it, said: "Am I blind? Perhaps. But not
so blind I'm unable to see that any mechanical psychoanalytic device is a useless crutch."

"Oh?" Kelexel found this an astonishing statement.
A useless crutch? The web? "You understand people
without such things, eh?" he asked.

"I've had a fair amount of success at it," Thurlow
said.

Kelexel took a step into the room, another. He
peered up at Thurlow. On the evidence, the native *did*
understand his own kind. Perhaps this wasn't an idle
boast. But could he also see into the Chem, understand
them? "What do you see in me?" he asked.

Thurlow studied the oddly squared-off, sensitive
face. There'd been pathos, a pleading in that question.
The answer must be gentle. "Perhaps," he said, "you've
played a part so long that you've almost *become* that
part."

Played a part? Kelexel wondered. He searched for
other meaning in the words. Nothing came to him. He
said: "My mechanical device has no human failures."

"How safe that must make the future," Thurlow
said. "How full of certainty. Then why are you here?"

Why am I here? Kelexel wondered. He could see now that the reasons he'd given himself were mere rationalizations. He began to regret this confrontation, felt a sense of naked exposure before Thurlow. "An immortal Chem doesn't have to give reasons," he said.

"Are you truly immortal?"

"Yes!"

Suddenly, Thurlow believed him without reservation. There was something about this intruder, some outrageous quality of person that belied pretense and sham. As abruptly, Thurlow realized why Kelexel had come here. Knowing this, he wondered how he could tell the creature.

"Immortal," Thurlow said. "I know why you're here. You're drunk on too much living. You're like a person climbing a sheer cliff. The higher you climb, the farther it is to fall—but oh how attractive the depths seem. You came here because you fear an accident."

Kelexel focused on the one word: *Accident!*

"There's no such thing as an accident for a Chem," he sneered. "The Chem is human and intelligent. Original intelligence may've been an accident, but nothing after that is an accident. Everything that happens to a Chem from the day he's taken from his vat is what he sets out to accomplish."

"How orderly," Thurlow said.

"Of course!"

"Such an ultimate neatness," Thurlow said. "When you do that to a garment, you take the life out of it. Neatness! Do that to a person and he'll live a life like an epigram . . . that's proved wrong after his death."

"But *we* do not die!"

Kelexel began to chuckle. This Thurlow was, after all, so transparent and easy to best in an argument. Kelexel controlled his chuckling, said: "We are mature beings who. . . ."

"You're not mature," Thurlow said.

Kelexel glared at him, remembering that Fraffin had said this same thing. "We *use* your kind for our amusement," he said. "We can live your lives vicariously without a. . . ."

"You came here to ask about death, to play with

death," Thurlow said, blurting it out. "You want to die and you're afraid to die!"

Kelexel swallowed, stared at Thurlow in shock. *Yes,* he thought. *That's why I'm here. And this witch doctor has seen through me.* Almost of itself, his head executed a betraying nod.

"Your mechanical device is a closed circle, a snake with its tail in its mouth," Thurlow said.

Kelexel found the will to protest: "We live forever by its psychological truth!"

"Psychological truth!" Thurlow said. "That's whatever you say it is."

"We're so far ahead of you primitive. . . ."

"Then why're you here asking help from a primitive?"

Kelexel shook his head. An oppressive sense of danger came over him. "You've never seen the web at work," he said. "How can you. . . ."

"I've seen you," Thurlow said. "And I know that any *school* based on mechanism is a closed circle of limited logic. The truth can't be enclosed in a circle. The truth's like countless lines radiating outward to take in a greater and ever greater space."

Kelexel felt himself fascinated by the movements of Thurlow's mouth. Scalding words dripped from that mouth. More than ever, Kelexel was sorry he'd come here. He could feel a shying away within himself, as though he stood before a closed door that might open any moment onto horror.

"In time, a curious thing happens to such schools," Thurlow said. "Your foundation philosophy begins to circle away from its original straight line. You're close at first. The error isn't recognized. You think you're still on course. And you swing farther and farther afield until the effort to devise new theorems to explain the preceding ones becomes more and more frantic."

"We're totally successful," Kelexel protested. "Your argument doesn't apply to us."

"Past success based on past truth isn't proof conclusive of a continuing success of continuing truth," Thurlow said. "We never actually attain a thing. We merely approach various conditions. Every word you've said about your Chem society betrays you. You think you have the ultimate answers. But *you* are here. You feel trapped. You know unconsciously that you're in a fixed system, unable to escape, forced to circle endlessly . . . until you fall."

"We'll never fall."

"Then why have you come to me?"

"I . . . I . . . ."

"People who follow a fixed system are like processional caterpillars," Thurlow said. "They follow the leader, always follow the leader, led on by the slime trail of the one ahead. But the leader comes on the trail of the last one in line and you're trapped. The trail grows thicker and thicker with your excrescence as you continue around and around the same path. And the excrescence is pointed out as verification that you're on the right track! You live forever! You're immortal!"

"We are!"

Thurlow lowered his voice, noting how Kelexel hung on every word. "And the path always appears straight," Thurlow said. "You see so little of it at a time, you don't notice when it curves back upon itself. You still see it as straight."

"Such wisdom!" Kelexel sneered. "It didn't save your precious madman, your precious Joe Murphey!"

Thurlow swallowed. *Why am I arguing with this creature?* he wondered. *What button did he push to set me going like this?*

"Did it?" Kelexel demanded, pressing his advantage.

Thurlow sighed. "Another vicious circle," he said. "We're still figuratively burning the Jews because they spread the plague. Each of us is both Cain and Abel. We throw stones at Murphey because he's the side we rejected. He was more Cain than Abel."

"You've a rudimentary sense of right and wrong," Kelexel said. "Was it wrong to . . . *extinguish* this Murphey?"

Oh, God! Thurlow thought. *Right and wrong! Nature and consequences!* "It's not a question of right and wrong!" he said. "This was a reaction right out of the depths. It was like . . . the tide . . . or a hurricane. It's . . . when it is, it *is!*"

Kelexel stared around the primitive room, noting the bed, the objects on the dresser—a picture of Ruth! How dare he keep a reminder of her? But who had better right? This room was a terrible, alien place suddenly. He wanted to be far away from it. But where could he go?

"You came here searching for a better psychological philosophy," Thurlow said, "not realizing that all such philosophies are blind alleys, little wormholes in an ancient structure."

"But you're . . . you're. . . ."

"Who should know more about such wormholes than one of the worms?" Thurlow asked.

Kelexel wet his lips with his tongue. "There must be perfection somewhere," he whispered.

"Must there? What would it be? Postulate a perfect psychology and an individual brought to perfection within such a system. You'd walk around in your never ending perfect circle until one day you found to your horror that the circle wasn't perfect! It can end!"

Kelexel became extremely conscious of every clock-ticking sound in the room.

"Extinction," Thurlow said. "Therein lies the end of your perfection, and fallacy in Eden. When your perfect psychology has cured your perfect subject, it still leaves him within the perfect circle . . . alone." He nodded. "And afraid." He studied Kelexel, noting how the creature trembled. "You came here because you're terrified by the thing that attracts you. You hoped I had some panacea, some primitive word of advice."

"Yes," Kelexel said. "But what could you have?" He blinked. "You're. . . ." He gestured at the room, unable to find words to express the poverty of this native's existence.

"You've helped me reach a decision and that's a great favor for which I thank you," Thurlow said. "If I was put here on earth to enjoy myself, that's what I intend to do. If I was put here at the whim of some superbeing who wants to watch me squirm—I'm not giving him the satisfaction!"

"Is there a superbeing?" Kelexel whispered. "What is there after . . . after. . . ."

"With such dignity as I can muster, I look forward to finding out . . . for myself," Thurlow said. "That's my choice, my decision. I think it'll leave me more time for living. I don't think time gives you any rest from this decision until you've made it."

Kelexel looked at his hands, the telltale fingernails, the puckered skin. "I live," he said. "Yet I live."

"But you haven't come to grips with the fact that all life's a *between* stage," Thurlow chided.

"Between?"

Thurlow nodded. He was speaking and acting from instinct now, fighting a danger whose shape he understood only vaguely. "Life's in motion," he said, "and there's just one big gamble—the living itself. Only an idiot fails to realize that a condemned man dies but once."

"But we don't die," Kelexel said, his voice pleading. "We never. . . ." He shook his head from side to side like a sick animal.

"Yet there's still that cliff you're climbing," Thurlow said. "And remember the attractive abyss."

Kelexel put his hands over his eyes. In his primitive and mysterious way, the witch doctor was right—hideously, implacably right.

A lurching motion behind Kelexel brought Thurlow's head snapping up, his eyes focused in shock as Ruth appeared there, supporting herself against the doorway. She flicked a glance across Thurlow, down to Kelexel.

"Ruth," Thurlow whispered.

Her red hair was piled high, tied with a glittering rope of green stones. Her body was covered by a long green robe belted by a golden-linked strand of square-cut crème-de-menthe jewels. There was an exotic strangeness about her that frightened Thurlow. He saw the bulge of her abdomen then beneath the jeweled belt, realized she was pregnant.

"Ruth," he said, louder this time.

She ignored him, concentrated her fury on Kelexel's back. "I wish you could die," she muttered. "Oh, how

I wish you could die. Please die, Kelexel. Do it for me. Die."

Kelexel lowered his hands from his face, turned with a slow dignity. Here she was at last, completely free, seeing him without any intervention from a manipulator. This was her reaction? This was the truth? He could feel Time running at its crazy Chem speed; all of his life behind him was a single heartbeat. She wanted him dead. A bile taste came into Kelexel's mouth. He, a Chem, had smiled on this mere native and she wanted him dead.

What he had planned for this moment stood frozen in his mind. It still could be done, but it wouldn't be a triumph. Not in Ruth's eyes. He raised a pleading hand to her, dropped it. What was the use? He could read the revulsion in her eyes. This was truth.

"Please die!" she hissed.

Thurlow, his face dark with anger, started across the room. "What have you done to her?" he demanded.

"You will stand where you are," Kelexel said, raising a palm toward Thurlow.

"Andy! Stop!" Ruth said.

He obeyed. There was controlled terror in her voice.

Ruth touched her abdomen. "This is what he did," she rasped. "And he killed my mother and my father and ruined you and. . . ."

"No violence, please," Kelexel said. "It's useless against me. I could obliterate you both so easily . . ."

"He could, Andy," Ruth whispered.

Kelexel focused on Ruth's bulging abdomen. Such an odd way to produce an offspring. "You don't wish me to obliterate your native friend?" he asked.

Mutely, she shook her head from side to side. God! What was the crazy little monster up to? There was such a feeling of terrible power in his eyes.

Thurlow studied Ruth. How weirdly exotic she appeared in that green robe and those big jewels. And pregnant! By this . . . this. . . .

"How odd it is," Kelexel said. "Fraffin believes you can be a control factor in our development, that we can aspire to a new level of being through you—perhaps even to maturity. It may be that he is more right than he knows."

Kelexel looked up as Thurlow skirted him, went to Ruth.

She pushed Thurlow's arm aside as he tried to put it around her shoulders. "What're you going to do, Kelexel?" she asked. Her voice held a thrumming quality, over-controlled.

"A thing no other immortal Chem has ever done," Kelexel said, realizing at last what had truly brought him here. And he wondered: *Have I the strength to do this?*

He turned his back on Ruth, crossed to Thurlow's bed, hesitated, smoothed the covers fastidiously. In that instant, the weight of all the Chem rested upon his shoulders, an ominous burden loaded with everything his kind refused to accept.

Seeing him at the bed, Ruth had the terrifying thought that Kelexel was about to impose the manipulator upon her, force Andy to watch them. *Oh God! Please, no!* she thought.

Kelexel turned back to them, sat on the edge of the bed. His hands rested lightly beside him. The bed felt soft, its covers warm and fuzzy. The bed gave off a stink of native perspiration which he found oddly erotic.

"What're you going to do?" Ruth whispered.

Kelexel thought: *I must not answer that question!* If he answered such questions, he knew his resolve might slip. He would do nothing important. He would accept the path of least resistance, the path which had lured his kind into their present stagnation.

"You will both stay where you are," Kelexel said.

He focused inward then, searched out the drumming center of his own heartbeat, thinking: *It should be possible. Rejuvination teaches us every nerve and muscle, every cell in our bodies. It should be possible.*

Thus far, his actions had no name except *it,* and he merely tested the possibilities. He concentrated on slowing his heartbeat.

At first, there was no reaction. But presently he sensed the beat slowing, almost imperceptibly, then, as he learned control, the pace slackened with a definite downward surge. He timed the rhythm to Ruth's breathing: inhale-one beat; exhale-one beat.

It skipped a beat!

Uncontrolled panic shot through Kelexel. He relaxed his grip on the heartbeat, fought to restore normality. *No!* he thought *That isn't what I want!* But another force had him now. Fear built on fear, terror on terror. Something gigantic and crushing gripped his chest. He could see the dark abyss, imagined Thurlow's cliff with himself upon its face clutching for any handhold, scrabbling to stay himself from that awful plunge.

Somewhere out in the foggy haze that had become his surroundings. Ruth's voice boomed at him: "Something's wrong with him!"

Kelexel realized he had fallen backward onto Thurlow's bed. The pain in his chest was a molten agony now. He could feel his heart laboring within that pain: beat-agony, beat-agony; beat-agony. . . .

Slowly, he felt his hands relaxing their grip on the face of the cliff. The abyss yawned. He felt that there was a real wind past his ears as he plunged into the darkness, turning, twisting. Ruth's voice wailed after him to become lost in emptiness: "My God! He's dying!"

Nothingness echoed upon nothingness and he thought he heard Thurlow's words: *"Delusion of grandeur."*

Thurlow rushed to the bed, felt for a pulse at Kelexel's temple. Nothing. The skin felt dry, smooth as metal. *Perhaps, they're not exactly like us,* he thought. *Maybe their pulse shows in another place.* He checked the right wrist. How limp and empty the hand felt! No pulse.

"Is he really dead?" Ruth whispered.

"I think he is." Thurlow dropped the flaccid hand, looked up at her. "You told him to die and he did."

A feeling oddly like remorse shot through her then. She thought of the Chem—immortal, all that seemingly endless living come to this. *Did I kill him?* she wondered. And aloud: "Did we kill him?"

Thurlow looked down at the still figure. He remembered the conversation with Kelexel, the Chem pleading for some kind of mystic reassurance from the primitive "witch doctor."

I gave him nothing, Thurlow thought.

"He was crazy," Ruth whispered. "They're all crazy."

Yes, this creature had a special kind of madness and it was dangerous, Thurlow told himself. *I was right to deny him. He was capable of killing us.*

All crazy? Thurlow wondered. He recalled Kelexel's brief recital of Chem society. There were more of the creatures then. What would they do if they found two *natives* with a dead Chem?

"Should we do something?" Ruth asked.

Thurlow cleared his throat. What did she mean? Artificial respiration, perhaps? But he sensed madness in such action. What did he know about Chem metabolism? Futility in his eyes, Thurlow looked up at Ruth and was just in time to see two more Chem press past her.

Ruth stood where the two Chem pushed her, obviously unable to move. Her face mirrored terror and defeat.

But the Chem acted as though they were alone in the room. They moved Kelexel's body on the bed.

Thurlow was caught by the tightly frozen looks on their faces. One, green-cloaked like Kelexel, was a bald, roundfaced female, her body solid and barrel-like. She bent over Kelexel with a gentle sureness, probing, palpitating. There was a feeling of professional sureness about her. The other, in a black cloak, had craggy features, a hooked nose. The skin of both was that weirdly metallic silver.

Not a word passed between them while the female made her examination.

Ruth stood watching as though nailed to the floor. The female was Ynvic, and Ruth remembered the sharp encounter with the shipsurgeon. The male Chem, though, was another matter, a person she'd seen only on the room screens as Kelexel talked to him—Fraffin the Director. Even Kelexel's tone had changed when speaking of Fraffin. Ruth knew she could never forget that haughty face. Here stood the embodiment of Chem power, the one who'd killed her parents to provide a brief amusement for his people. He'd killed countless humans for no better reason. His acts transcended brutality to a point where they no longer could be called brutal. They were acts of casual expediency, less direct even than stepping on an ant.

Presently, Ynvic straightened, spoke in shiptongue: "He has done it. He has certainly done it." There was a blank emptiness in her voice.

The sound was gibberish to Thurlow, but he sensed the horror.

To Ruth, a product of storyship education imprinters, the words were as clear as English, but there were overtones of meaning which escaped her.

Ynvic turned to stare at Fraffin. The look that passed between them was filled with the poignancy of defeat. They both knew what had really happened here.

Fraffin sighed, shuddered. The blurred-off moment of Kelexel's death had come to him through Tiggywaugh's web, the Chem oneness momentarily shattered by that impossible demarcation. Feeling that death, sensing its direction, Fraffin had known the identity with terrifying sureness. Every Chem in the universe had felt it, of course, and turned in this direction, no doubt, but Fraffin knew that few had shared his certain knowledge of identity. It was as though he'd anticipated the event.

Dying, Kelexel had defeated him. Fraffin had known this even as he dashed with Ynvic for a flitter and homed on this point in space. The sky up there was full of craft from the storyship, all of the crewmen afraid to come closer. Most of them had guessed who'd died here, Fraffin realized. They knew the Primacy wouldn't rest until it identified the dead one. No Chem out there would rest until the mystery was solved.

Here was the first immortal Chem to die, the first in all that crazy endless Time. This planet would soon be aswarm with the Primacy's minions, all the storyship's secrets exposed.

Wild Chem! It'd be an emotional blast through the

Chem universe. There was no telling what might be done with these creatures.

"What . . . killed him?" Ruth ventured, speaking shiptongue.

Ynvic turned a glassy stare on her. The poor stupid female! What could she know of Chem ways? "He killed himself," Ynvic said, her voice soft. "It's the only way a Chem can die."

"What're they saying?" Thurlow asked. He heard his voice come out overloud. "He killed himself," Ruth said. "That's the only way a Chem can die . . ."

Ruth heard herself translating as though it were another person revealing this to some part of her which had been sleeping. *The only way a Chem can die . . .*

Fraffin, hearing the exchange, felt the need to speak lest he fall into an abyss which lay within his own skull. He spoke in English to Thurlow: "It has never happened before. A Chem has never died before."

Thurlow absorbed this and thought: *You're mistaken. You have to be mistaken.* There would've been other Chem deaths . . . long ago. Otherwise these Chem could not be what they obviously were—fugitives. They were fugitives from death. Thurlow almost spoke this thought, but he saw that Fraffin had fallen into a reverie approaching trance. The female Chem had finished examining the body on the bed and was staring at her companion.

Presently, Ynvic spoke in shiptongue: "It was the only way he could defeat us."

Fraffin nodded, hearing Ynvic as though from a distance. *What a price to pay for victory.* What a story it would've made for the empatheaters of the Chem universe! For a Chem to kill himself . . . Fraffin looked at Ruth, beautiful, exotic creature. He felt an abrupt communication with her and with all the others like her. *They have no past except the past I gave them.* The thought was filled with despairing pride. He knew he had lost his world. Kelexel . . . the Primacy had won. And not one among that Primacy could really know *what* they had won.

His nostrils were suddenly filled with the same smell

of bitter salt he'd inhaled once in the sistral winds of Carthage. He felt his own life identified with Carthage.

The Primacy would exile him to lonely, Chemless foreverness, he knew. It was the only punishment they could inflict on a fellow Chem, no matter what the crime.

How long will I be able to withstand it before I take Kelexel's way out? he wondered.

Again, he inhaled the dusty, salt smell—Carthage, leafless, contaminated, stripped in the blaze-light of Cato's gloating, its survivors crouching, terrified.

"I told you it'd end this way," Ynvic said.

Fraffin closed his eyes against the sight of her. In his self-imposed darkness, he could see his own future: the eagle's eyrie come to shame, hidden in a dooryard. He could see it by the dark of the blood that fed the ravenous oracle within him. They'd fit him with every machine and device for comfort and foreverness—everything except a fellow Chem or any other living creature.

He imagined an automatic toaster erupting and himself begging life into it. His thoughts were like a skipped rock touching the surface of a lake. His memories of this planet would not let him alone. *He* was the skipped rock, condensing eons: A tree, a face ... the glimpse of a face, and his memory shaped out Kallima-Sih's daughter given in marriage (at a Chem's direction) to Amenophis III three thousand five hundred puny year-beats ago.

And facts: he remembered that King Cyrus had preferred archeology to the throne. The fool!

And places: a wall in a dirty village along a desert track, a place called Muqayyar. One wall and it called up mighty Ur as he had seen it last. ... In his mind, Tiglath-Pileser was not gone, but marched yet before the Chem recorders, through Ishtar Gate, along Procession Street. It was a timeless parade with Sennacherib, Shalmanessar, Isem-Dagan, Sinsarra-iskun, all dancing to the Chem tune.

There was a worldpulse in Fraffin's mind now, a sinepounding timewave: diastole/systole, compelling blacksnake ripples that whipped across generations.

His thoughts dipped briefly into the Babylonian Lingua-franca that had served the merchant world for two thousand years before he'd stirred the pot by giving them Jesus.

Fraffin felt then that his own mind was the sole repository for his creatures, his person the only preservation they had—a place of yearnings, full of voices and faces and entire races whose passage had left no mark except distantly outraged whispering . . . and tears. And all of it played only in his own memories. That was the only empatheater left to him: the awareness within his own head. These thoughts produced a terminal flare of consciousness so that he saw then something of what Kelexel had seen in those final moments.

Again, he looked at Ruth . . . at Thurlow. Their fear lay so obvious upon their features. Fraffin felt his mind spinning. This, he knew, had to be the making of maturity for himself. And after maturity . . .

I'm seeing life from their point of view! he thought. *I've become one of my own creatures!*

All the history of this planet . . . *his* planet lay collapsed and condensed now within him.

From Sheba's time his memory handed him a vision of her camel-station metropolis, a place that withstood Aelius Gallus and his legions, but now like Carthage and himself was reduced to petty walls of crumbled dust, kitchen middens, sandspume, silent stones—a place waiting for some King Cyrus with shovels to expose its empty skulls.

Aurum et ferrum, he thought. *Gold and iron.*

And he wondered if there'd be a wink-flare of reason before the burning darkness.

I'll have no activity in which to hide my mind, he thought, *nothing at last to protect me from boredom.*

Epilogue

BY ORDER OF THE PRIMACY:

No further applications will be taken during this cycle from persons wishing to observe the wild Chem in their native habitat. Applications for the next cycle will be taken only from observers qualified in genetics, sociology, philosophy and Chem history and their related fields.

Applications for interviews with the native witch doctor, Androclesthurlow, and his mate, Ruth, are subject to the following restrictions:

1) Interviewer is prohibited from discussing mortality.

2) Interviewer is prohibited from discussing the punishment of Director Fraffin, Shipsurgeon Ynvic or their storyship crewmembers.

3) Interviewer may not question the native female on her relationship with Investigator Kelexel.

4) All interviews must be conducted at the witch doctor's hut on the native reserve planet under the usual security limitations.

Be it noted that no requests to adopt wild Chem infants from the native reserve planet or the seeded planets can be honored until completion of studies upon the offspring of Kelexel and the native female. Studies and tests of selected wild Chem infants are now being conducted and results will be announced when those studies are completed.

For security reasons, all unauthorized attempts to visit the native reserve planet are subject to severe punishment.

(SEALED THIS DAY IN THE NAME OF THE PRIMACY)

DEL REY GOLD SEAL SELECTIONS... SCIENCE FICTION CLASSICS IN QUALITY PAPER-BACK EDITIONS.

Major works of imaginative fiction that have become modern literary classics.